Praise for Val Griswold-Ford's *Winter Secrets*:

*"Griswold-Ford cooks a story as sweet as peppermint cookies in a
Christmas stocking. You'll gobble it right up!"*

-**Tamara Siler Jones**, author of the
Dubric Byerly Mysteries, Bantam Spectra

A Carter's Cove Advent Story

Winter Secrets

VAL GRISWOLD-FORD

ALSO BY VAL GRISWOLD-FORD

Available from Dragon Moon Press

The Dark Horseman Trilogy
Not Your Father's Horseman
Dark Moon Seasons
Last Rites

The Complete Guide to Writing Fantasy series
(with Tee Morris and Lai Zhao)
Alchemy with Words
The Opus Magnus
The Author's Grimoire

Rum & Runestones (editor)
Spells & Swashbucklers (editor)

Available from Captain's Table Press

Snow (A Dark Horseman Novella)
Convoy (A True Souls Short Story)
Into Thin Air (A Pendragon Casefiles Novella)

Available from ImagineThat! Studios

"The Sun Never Sets" *(A Tale from the Archives short story)*

A Carter's Cove Advent Story

Winter Secrets

VAL GRISWOLD-FORD

DARKER
REALITY
DRS
STUDIOS

A **Darker Reality Studios** Novel

Published in the United States of America
by Darker Reality Studios
www.DarkerReality.com

Copyright © 2016 by Val Griswold-Ford
www.VG-Ford.com
and
Darker Reality Studios

Cover design and cover art by Starla Huchton
Designed By Starla (www.DesignedByStarla.com)

Cover layout, interior illustrations, interior layout,
and book design by Scott E. Pond
Scott E. Pond Designs, LLC (www.scottpond.com)

Edited by Sue Baiman
(www.MyEditorIsSue.com)

Library of Congress Cataloging-in-Publication Data
Griswold-Ford, Val
Winter Secrets / / Val Griswold-Ford.—1st ed.
p. cm.
1. Fantasy—Fiction

ISBN: 978-1-944672-02-7

PRINTED IN THE UNITED STATES OF AMERICA
10 9 8 7 6 5 4 3 2 1

FIRST EDITION: May 2016

To Mom, who asked for a Christmas story.
Carter's Cove wouldn't exist without you.

I miss you.

Acknowledgments

Thank you to my amazing editor, Sue Baiman, who took a great story and made it shine. You helped me find even more in the Cove to tell.

Thank you also to all the writers who encouraged me to write this silly little story that was so far outside my comfort zone that it wasn't funny. Especially my writer's group (Kathy, Kiaya, Barbara, LJ, Sarge, Mike, Rob, Jess, Donna), who kept me on task (mostly).

Thank you to Starla Hutchton, for the amazing cover that brought the Cove to life.

Thank you to Scott Pond, for giving me the opportunity to get this out to a larger audience by starting his own press.

And thank you to my wonderful husband, Brian, who told me to go and write more times than I can remember. I love you, babe.

- Val Griswold-Ford

Author Note

When I was a child, Christmas was a big deal in my family (let's be honest – it still is). My father was a sailor in the US Navy, and he wasn't always home during the year, but he was ALWAYS home for at least part of Christmas. My mother was raised Jewish, and so Christmas was something she didn't celebrate until she married my dad. We didn't spend Christmas Eve with anyone but family – we did a buffet at home, watched an old VHS tape of the Nutcracker Ballet with Baryshnikov and Kirkland, opened a small gift, and went to bed. I adored it. I still do.

One of the big December traditions in our house was the Advent Calendar. After Thanksgiving, we would pull out the Christmas box from the crawlspace, and the Advent Calendar would go up on the wall next to the front door. It was a big Victorian house, with a room for every day of the month of December, and it came with a paper Santa Claus. On December 1, he would climb down the chimney, and each morning, we would move him one room closer to the big Christmas tree in the parlor. That Advent Calendar is long gone, but I still remember it fondly every year as the season comes around.

In 2010, I decided that I wanted to do my own Advent Calendar to share with my friends and family. However, I'm not a graphic artist. I'm a writer. So I decided to do an Advent story instead, and post a little bit more to my blog every day. That's how Carter's Cove was born.

I had no idea that this little story would grow so much, and that Schrodinger, Molly and the other inhabitants of the Cove would have such a following. But since they have, I've decided to revise and release the stories as books that you can read to your heart's content. The title of each chapter in this first book is the carol that

Molly received on that day.

Thank you for sharing this journey with me, and I hope you continue to enjoy the world of Carter's Cove. Merry Christmas, one and all.

Winter Secrets

We Need a Little Christmas
Wednesday, December 1

*M**erry Christmas!*

Molly Barrett opened her hazel eyes a crack, just enough to see the furry face grinning a satisfied feline grin at her in the twilight of her bedroom. She turned her head and squinted at the alarm clock on her nightstand. Ten minutes before 5 a.m. She groaned and looked back at Schrodinger. "Are you seriously planning on doing this every morning this month?"

Lily and Jack say that you have to greet the morning with Merry Christmas during December, Schrodinger told her, butting her cheek gently with the top of his head. *So Santa knows you believe.* The soft fur made her smile, despite the time.

"Yes, but does it have to be before the alarm goes off?"

Oh. Schrodinger hung his head for a moment. *They did say that if we do it first thing, we won't forget it!*

"Lily is four, and Jack is a half blue-tick hound, half-German Shepherd mix," Molly said, heaving the 28-pound CrossCat off her chest with both hands. She stretched, turned the alarm off, and then continued, "You really want to take their advice on this?"

Schrodinger looked up at her from the tangle of blankets he'd landed on. *Well, they do say that the children know Santa the best,* he said, after a moment. *And I really want to make sure Santa comes this year!*

"Why wouldn't he?" Molly said, running her fingers through her dark hair, noting absently that it was getting long again.

You never know, and I don't want to take that chance.

She started to respond as she got out of bed, then the image of what her brother and sister-in-law must be going through flashed through her mind. Schrodinger was only 28 pounds, and he knew how to control his paws. Jack was at least 90 pounds, and like most young dogs, had more enthusiasm than brains. So all she said was, "I don't mind the greeting. It was the landing on my chest ten minutes before the alarm went off that startled me."

I'm sorry. I'll check the clock tomorrow, the CrossCat said, following her into the kitchen. Molly's apartment was on the second floor of an old brownstone in the heart of Carter's Cove: it contained two bedrooms (one of which was piled high with boxes and odds and ends), a living room with a working fireplace, a kitchen with enough room to hold a small dining table and chairs at one end of it, and a bathroom – all she and Schrodinger needed. Occasionally her mother suggested she might want to buy a house, rather than rent, but Molly didn't see the need. She liked her little apartment. And houses were expensive to maintain.

She hit the start button on the coffeemaker on the counter and inhaled the fragrant scent of cloves and almonds as tea began to bubble down into the large pot, once again blessing the forethought that had her setting up everything for the morning caffeine she needed before she went to bed. "Why are you so obsessed with Santa Claus? It's not like you don't get spoiled rotten by everyone anyways. And he's never not come to the Cove."

I don't want him to come for me, Schrodinger said, jumping up into one of the chairs and waiting patiently for her to heat water for him. He preferred Earl Grey to her favorite Christmas tea for his first mug of the day. Molly took his mug (a large cappuccino mug, so he could drink without issue) from the drainboard, filled it with water, and then held it between her hands for a moment. The water boiled, and she put a teabag in, then set it on the table in front of Schrodinger. *And this is my very first Christmas, so I want to do it right. CrossCats don't celebrate Christmas, and Santa has never come to the Den.*

"Really?" Molly blinked. "Do you celebrate anything?"

Yes, but it's closer to Yule, or the Winter Solstice. The name doesn't really translate well. He dipped his tongue delicately into his tea. *But it's a time when everyone in the Den comes together. And there are usually gifts.*

"Won't you miss it this year?"

I don't know yet, he said, cocking his head. *I hadn't really thought of it. I'm too excited about celebrating here.*

"Okay. So why are you obsessed with Santa coming, if you don't want him to bring you a present?" Molly opened the fridge, wondering what to make for breakfast now that the tea was almost done.

I want him to bring you someone special, silly. You deserve it.

Molly paused, her hand resting on the fridge's handle, and blinked. "What?"

Schrodinger didn't answer her immediately, but after another mouthful of tea, he said, *I want him to bring someone special for you, because you deserve it, and I don't want you to be lonely anymore. Lily said if I was good all year, and I have been, and I'm extra-good this month, Santa will bring me everything I wish for. And I wish for someone who makes you happy, because that would make me happy.*

Abandoning the fridge, Molly went over to the table and hugged the ocelot-sized CrossCat to her. "You are my best friend," she said, emotion tightening her throat. "What would I do without you? You're the only Christmas present I need. We don't need anyone else." Especially not after the last person she'd let into her life. Molly pushed the image of her ex-boyfriend firmly from her mind.

He purred, and the sound vibrated through her. *Not that I object, but you need someone human to love as well.* Then he butted his head against hers playfully and added, *And I need someone else to keep the bed warm. My feet get cold, you know.*

"Ah-ha! The truth comes out!" Molly squeezed him again and

then got up to pour herself a mug of tea before going back to looking at the contents of her fridge. "So tell me, Schrodinger, did you have someone picked out? Or were you leaving that up to Santa?"

Up to Santa. His tea done, Schrodinger began to clean his whiskers. *I'm still new to the Cove, after all. And I'm just a CrossCat. But if you want a suggestion for breakfast, I think bacon and eggs sound wonderful.*

"Just what did you eat before you moved in with me?" Molly asked, laughing as she pulled a package of bacon and the carton of eggs from the fridge.

Whatever was available. We're flexible creatures.

Later, after breakfast and a quick shower, she and Schrodinger walked out into the crisp morning air, Molly carrying a large cooler full of cookie dough over one shoulder. She'd spent most of the prior evening mixing the peppermint-laced dough; once she got to work, the ovens would go on, and CrossWinds Books would smell amazing.

She loved her job. Most of her college classmates had wondered why Molly hadn't taken her degree in culinary studies from Johnson and Wales and her near-mythical prowess in a kitchen and gone to cook in some Michelin-starred restaurant anywhere she wanted. Instead, she'd come back home to Carter's Cove and opened a small tea shop within the bookstore her Aunt Margie owned. It was something that she knew her classmates would never understand. Carter's Cove, with the scents of magic and the sea combining in the air, was the only place the young kitchen witch wanted to be.

Besides, by running the tea shop, she got to cook and feed people (which she adored), but without the headaches of running a restaurant in a busy city. The Cove was quiet, moving at a slow small-town pace. The tea shop offered pots of tea, cookies, and whatever else she felt like baking that day, served in a little tea room that held six tables. She worked five days a week, closing the kitchen on Tuesdays and Thursdays (although there were always cookies and muffins in the fridge, and a kettle on the stove, and Aunt Margie or DC, the head clerk at the bookstore, could usually be wheeled into providing tea and food), and Molly could bring Schrodinger in to work with her. *Honestly, what more could I ask for?*

Schrodinger's wish came back to her and she sighed. Her love life hadn't gone quite as well as her professional life had. *Oh, well,* she thought privately. *Maybe it just isn't the right time yet. It's not as if I'm unhappy where I am now.*

Snow crunched under her boots as they walked briskly down Center Street towards Main Street and the storefronts. It was a short walk from the brownstone to the bookstore even in winter, which meant she didn't need a car. Carter's Cove was huddled under a new white cover; the snowflakes had come down thick and fast the night before, and Molly could taste more on the still air. "It's going to be a long winter," she said.

Only as long as the last one.

Molly chuckled. The CrossCat was amazingly literal when he wanted to be.

When will the lights go on? Schrodinger asked her, as they turned the corner onto Main Street and headed for the bookstore. It was still early; no hint of sunrise stained the eastern edge of the sky yet and stars twinkled in the darkness above them.

"Not until tonight, when we walk home," Molly said. "They shut them off at 4 am, I think." She squinted up at the snowflake that was attached to one of the light posts. "Although the last week before Christmas, they leave them on all night."

That will be awesome.

At this hour of the morning, the traffic consisted of herself, Schrodinger, and Sergeant Jamie Ford on his way into the police station. He waved to them and slowed the cruiser down. "Morning, Molly, Schrodinger!" he called through his open window. "What's the special cookie today?"

"Peppermint candy canes, since it's the start of the Christmas season," Molly said, and grinned when he gave her a thumbs up. "I'll put some aside for you, then?"

"My hero! I'll be in after school with Sarah. We'll see you then!" Jamie waved again and drove off slowly into the dawn.

Schrodinger's ears perked up. *Sarah?* The little blind ten-year-old was one of his favorite people, especially since she loved to read to him.

"That's what he said." Molly picked her way carefully up the stairs to the front door of CrossWinds Books, hoping the boy Aunt Margie had hired to shovel would be there before he went to school. *Then again, it's barely 6:30,* she reminded herself. *Not everyone is up at this hour.*

She finally found the correct key, looked up at the door to insert it in the lock, and frowned.

Aunt Margie had already hung the festive holly wreath that had adorned the oak and glass door of the bookstore for as long as Molly could remember. This morning, stuck among the glossy dark leaves and crimson berries, was a small red envelope with "Molly" written on it in elaborate script.

What's that? Schrodinger put his front paws up on her leg and stood up, trying to see what had stopped her. Molly set the cooler down on the top step and plucked the envelope from the wreath. It slid out easily. Heavier than she expected, though, as if there was something more than just a card in it.

"I don't know," she said, unlocking the door and opening it. Schrodinger bounded in ahead of her as she carried the cooler in and relocked the door. Then Molly shut off the alarm and went into the back of the building where her spotless kitchen awaited her.

Aunt Margie had redesigned the entire store after Molly came back to the Cove and laid out her plans. Now, instead of one large open space downstairs filled with bookshelves, the bottom back half of the store held Molly's kitchen and the small tea room, which contained a wood stove as well as the tables. In addition, there were overstuffed chairs with small end tables next to them scattered around the larger room upstairs. Technically, Molly only dealt with the tea room, but everyone knew they could take tea anywhere. Most of the regulars had a tab running and paid their bills monthly. People told DC what they'd eaten or drunk as they left, and Molly didn't have to worry about it. The only rule was that if you spilled something on the books, you'd just bought them. No one had complained yet.

Molly set the cooler on the island in the kitchen and laid the mysterious envelope next to it. Her fingers itched to open it, but Molly had a routine, and she didn't like to disrupt it. It threw off her whole day. First, she went into the tea room and lit the wood stove, then she checked the pile of wood next to it, to make sure she had enough for the day. After she made sure the flames were dancing, she went back to the kitchen and set the large copper kettle on its designated burner, turned on the small stereo (set to WCOV, which was playing Christmas carols, of course), and started her ovens preheating. Then she pulled out cookie sheets and set them on the long counter on the outside wall of the kitchen, laying silicone mats on them.

Pulling the first bundle of dough from the cooler, Molly lost herself in the familiar rhythms, humming along with the carols as she rolled out long logs of red and white dough, then twisted them together and shaped them into candy canes. Only when the first batch of cookies was in the oven and a second set lay ready to go did she pour herself and Schrodinger a cup of tea.

"Schrodinger? Want to come and see what the envelope has in it?" she called out, and the CrossCat immediately stuck his mackerel-striped face around the corner of the kitchen door. "I know, I know. Silly question. Come on in, I'm opening it now. I have tea for you too."

He slipped in through the doorway and jumped lightly onto one of the stools, a trick he'd mastered in the first few days he'd come in with her. She sat on one next to him, set the two mugs down, and picked up the envelope. Sliding one finger under the flap, Molly broke the seal and poured the contents carefully into her hand: a mini CD in a jewel case, and a scrap of what she was pretty sure was parchment. On it was more of the lovely calligraphy that graced the envelope itself.

What does it say? Schrodinger asked, leaning over and almost putting his paw in his tea. *Who's it from?*

"I don't know," Molly said, turning the scrap over in her hand, looking for clues. There were none, and she read the brief message out loud: "To Molly. You need a little Christmas joy, and I'm the one to give it to you. Love, SA"

SA? Santa? It must be Santa! Schrodinger bounced like a small child, his ears flattening back in excitement, and nearly fell off his stool.

"Easy!" Molly laughed, as he scrabbled to remain in place. "Don't fall. Shouldn't it be SC, for Santa Claus?"

Maybe he's trying to be anonymous?

Molly laughed again. "I'm not convinced. Let's see what's on this CD."

She got up and pulled the little CD from its case, then put it in the top of the stereo. After a few minutes, the lilting strains of "We Need a Little Christmas" filled the kitchen, and she grinned. "We need a little Christmas indeed. Whoever SA is, at least he has good taste."

"What are you listening to?"

The question cut across the music, and Molly and Schrodinger both turned to see the owner of CrossWinds Books in the doorway to the kitchen. "Good morning, Aunt Margie!" Molly said. "Ready for your morning cup?" She didn't wait for an answer, but went to get another mug and her aunt's favorite spicy black Assam.

Margie Barrett, a short, plump woman with a kind face and dark curls clustered about her head, stood still, a delighted smile playing on her lips as she listened to the song. "I haven't heard that version in years," she said, coming in to the kitchen as the song ended. She accepted the mug from Molly, as well as a kiss on her cheek, and sank on the stool her niece had vacated. "Where did you find it?"

"Someone left it for me on the front door." Molly filled her in on how she and Schrodinger had found the mysterious envelope. "So now you know as much as we do," she concluded, pulling a batch of cookies from the oven, and then putting another set of pans in.

I think it's from Santa, Schrodinger confided, draining his tea cup. *I checked all around the store, and there's nothing else strange here! Nothing was disturbed. Only Santa could do that!*

"Hard to argue with that logic," Aunt Margie agreed, her hazel eyes sparkling. "I might have another explanation, though, based on the note."

Really? Both Schrodinger and Molly looked at Aunt Margie.

"I don't know if it's right, but when I was younger, SA meant Secret Admirer," Aunt Margie told them. "Uncle Art spent one whole summer leaving messages for me signed SA, because he was too shy to tell me in person. Maybe someone's got their eyes on Molly, and are just working up the nerve to talk to her."

"Seriously?" Molly laughed. "I doubt it. There's no one here who would be interested in me."

Schrodinger looked from her to Aunt Margie and then back. *But why would they not sign it with their names? How are you supposed to know who it is?*

"That's part of the fun," Aunt Margie said. "Figuring the mystery out. It's also a way to break the ice with someone you might not know well."

Which is why Molly was skeptical, although she'd thought of a secret admirer as well when she'd first read the note. She knew just about everyone in the Cove, and most of the guys considered her a sister, not a girlfriend. One of the hazards of coming back to one's hometown.

"Don't worry," she said, starting to roll out more dough. "I'm sure we'll figure it out."

Aunt Margie stood up, taking her tea with her. "Let me know if you get any more special deliveries. You know how much I love a good mystery."

White Christmas
Thursday, December 2

Thursdays were Molly and Schrodinger's second day off during the week, and they usually enjoyed sleeping in. Molly had successfully convinced Schrodinger that he didn't have to greet her as soon as the morning hit – as long as they said "Merry Christmas" to each other when they woke up, Santa would be pleased. Sarah had agreed with Molly when she'd come in later, to Molly's relief.

Thus, it was nearly 9 am when she finally wandered into the kitchen and started her tea pot. Schrodinger followed her, and she made breakfast leftover omelets for the two of them while the tea brewed. Then she finally looked out the window. "Oh lord, cat, it's a good thing we didn't have any plans to go out today."

It was white out – tiny white snowflakes, falling fast and furious to land on the already frozen ground atop the snow that had fallen on Thanksgiving. Carter's Cove, situated on the coast of Maine, usually enjoyed a white Christmas, but this looked to be a record year for snowfall. Which could be good, or bad, depending on the way it came. And when.

"Maybe we can make a snowman in the backyard today," she said to Schrodinger, who had started his after-breakfast bath. "It could be fun, and I think I have an old hat we can use."

Is it the right kind of snow, though? He looked at the flakes shushing against the window glass, whiskers twitching as he considered the idea. *It feels like it might be too cold to stick together well. Too dry. Not like over Thanksgiving, when we built the snowman at Lily's.*

"We can check when we go get the mail. If it's not the right kind of snow, maybe we'll make snowman cookies for the cafe tomorrow. I've still got cookie dough that didn't get dyed the other day in the fridge." She watched the snow come down, liking the idea of the cookies more and more. "There's fondant in the fridge too, so we could make a little display, maybe. A snowball fight. Have you ever had a snowball fight, Schrodinger?"

It's rather hard to throw snowballs with paws, he said dryly, looking up at her. *But Lily threw them for Jack and I. Why?*

"My brother Nathan and I used to have snowball fights all the time with our friends. I don't think I've had one since college, though," she said, cupping her tea mug in her hand. "Or skating or sledding or anything fun like that. Riding in a sleigh and singing Christmas carols while looking at the lights."

Why not?

"Why not what?"

Why haven't you gone to do those things? Schrodinger rearranged himself on the chair, his tail wrapped around his paws. *They sound like a lot of fun.*

"They were," Molly agreed. "I don't know. We've all been so busy the last couple of years around this time of year. I was working to get the tea shop off the ground, and Tom..." She trailed off, and shook her head. "Tom wasn't really the type to do things like that. So I stopped doing them."

Schrodinger's paw reached over and laid softly on her arm. *But he's not here anymore, and I like to do new things,* he said. *After all, this is my first Christmas.*

"It is," she said, and smiled at him, laying one hand on his paw. "And so one of these nights, we'll have to get the gang together and go caroling."

Caroling? What's that?

"It's singing Christmas carols. Dr. Robbins, the old vet, hitches his horses Daisy and Shredder to his sleigh and gives rides to anyone who wants. The only charge is apples or carrots for the horses." She chuckled ruefully. "He'd load all of us when we were kids: me, Nathan, Sue, Lai, Noemi, Luke, even Tom sometimes, and some poor adult who'd been roped into chaperoning us. We would go around our neighborhood and sing at all the homes, and people would give us cookies and cider and hot chocolate. Probably to get us to stop, honestly. Lai has a good voice, but the rest of us were more enthusiastic than anything else. Doc probably wore earplugs under his earmuffs."

Do you think we can go again? It sounds like fun!

"It was," Molly said. The snow shushed against the window, the barest sound breaking through the silence of the small town. The plows hadn't gone by in a while, and the world outside their warm kitchen lay blanketed in icy white, with no one venturing into the storm. "I'm sure we can get the girls together, at the very least. And maybe we'll take Lily and Jack."

The more she thought about it, the more she liked that idea. The last few years had seen Christmas be more work than fun, and no small part of that had come from the fact that Tom Alward, her boyfriend, hadn't enjoyed Christmas or really anything that forced him to deal with his family. So she'd fallen out of the habit of the season. *Time to change that…*

They sat together in companionable silence, watching the snow fall and drinking tea. The minutes ticked by, but Molly didn't care – she hadn't planned anything more strenuous than addressing the few Christmas cards she normally sent to some of her old friends who lived elsewhere. *Although that snowball fight scene does sound like fun to make, and I need to use that fondant anyways…*

By 11 a.m., though, she'd managed to get herself dressed enough to go down and shovel the walk, only to discover that her downstairs neighbor Henry had beaten her to it. Schrodinger had declined her invitation to join her in the chore, pointing out that he would keep her couch warm and from wandering off when her back was turned. As apparently it was wont to do, although she'd never noticed it.

Henry had even sanded the flagstones, and the snowfall had lessened to random flurries, so Molly decided to check her mailbox before going back upstairs to bake. Some of those snowmen cookies would find their way to the young night watchman who lived below her, in thanks.

The brilliant red envelope stuck out from the mailbox's dim interior like a stoplight, and Molly paused, a little chilled. *Who is sending these? How do they know where I live?* Then she shook her head as her common sense reasserted itself. *It's not that big a town, silly. Everyone in the Cove knows where you live.*

She pulled the envelope out with the other mail and looked closely at it. Her name, in the same gorgeous flowing script, winked up at her in the dim daylight. Metallic ink, she realized. Someone was putting a lot of effort into this.

"Christmas cards already? Damn, someone's on the ball." The comment shattered the silence, and Molly looked up to see the tall, rangy figure of Drew McIntyre, one of the newest members to Carter's Cove. He was striding up the sidewalk towards her holding a small tablet, his boots crunching through the snow, his dark hair covered with a knit cap that matched his green mittens. He grinned at her, then the grin faded when she didn't immediately return it. "Is everything okay, Molly?"

She smiled then, not only to reassure him, but herself. "Yeah, just finding myself with a bit of a mystery." Offering him the envelope as he joined her, she continued, "This is the second envelope someone's sent to me. Whoever it is left the first one on the wreath at the bookstore for me to find yesterday morning. Weird, huh?"

Drew turned the envelope over, hefting it. "Definitely weird. The calligraphy is beautiful, though. What's inside?"

"If it's the same as yesterday, a mini CD with a Christmas carol on it," Molly told him, flushing a little. Tom would have looked down almost pityingly at her for that.

"Someone's sending you Christmas carols? That's awesome!" Drew surprised her by throwing his head back and laughing in delight. It was a hearty, unselfconscious laugh that bounced off the nearby buildings, and Molly couldn't help but join in.

"You don't think it's weird, though?" she asked, as they subsided into giggles.

"Of course it's weird, but in a neat sort of way." He handed her back the envelope. "It's like this whole town – weird, in an awesomely neat way. It's so different from the way Marionville was. Are you going to open it now?"

"If I open it down here, Schrodinger will kill me because he won't get to see what it is." Molly turned back to her door, then looked back at him. "Are you in a hurry? If not, come on up and we'll see what SA has sent me this time."

"I can take a few minutes," Drew said, tucking the tablet in his coat pocket and following her up the walk. "SA?"

"Yes, that's how yesterday's note was signed." Molly filled him in as they went up the stairs, pausing on the landing outside her door on the second floor to pull off her boots before they went in to her apartment. Drew had only moved to the Cove a few months before, right around Halloween, but he wasn't considered an outsider, really. Not like the tourists that came through to look at the quaint New England harbor town. Then again, Drew had come from a Crossroads town in out in the Midwest. Crossroads folks tended to stick together.

"So why were you walking down our sidewalk?" Molly asked him as they went in to her apartment. "Not that I mind seeing you, but aren't you supposed to be at the Station right now?"

Drew made a face and started to reply, then stumbled backwards and fell over, knocked down by an enthusiastic CrossCat shouting, *Drew! Drew! Merry Christmas!*

"Merry Christmas to you too," Drew wheezed, trying without

success to suck more air into his lungs. The problem was Schrodinger, who had ended up on top of his chest. Molly tried to move him, but she was laughing so hard that her efforts to shift the CrossCat failed for the first few moments. Eventually, she got Schrodinger to move and offered Drew a hand up.

"Sorry," she said, using her other hand to wipe tears of mirth from her eyes. "It's his first Christmas and he's a little obsessed."

It's for a good cause! If I wish everyone a Merry Christmas, and I'm good, Santa will bring me the best present ever! Schrodinger said.

"Oh?" Drew said, taking a seat at the dining room table. "And what would that be?"

"Schrodinger, look, I got another envelope!" Molly said hastily, trying to distract the CrossCat before he said any more.

It worked, to her relief. Schrodinger zeroed in on her, Drew's question forgotten. *Is it from him? From Santa?*

"Let's see. It looks the same." Molly slipped one finger under the flap of the envelope and slid it open. As she'd expected, there was another mini CD inside, along with another scrap of paper, and a shower of glittery snowflakes that exploded across the floor.

Snow! Just like outside! Schrodinger said, batting at some of it.

Molly handed the parchment to Drew while she put the CD into the CD player on the table.

"Dear Molly, I hope you like the snow as much as I do. It's so pretty! SA," Drew read out, and then, as if on cue, the sounds of "White Christmas" filled the kitchen.

It has to be Santa! Schrodinger said, dancing through the glittery confetti, spreading it around him. *After all, he loves snow!*

"He does," Molly agreed. "But then why isn't it SC, not SA?" She looked over at Drew. "Aunt Margie thinks I have a secret admirer."

"I can see that." Drew nodded. "But I guess Santa's a valid theory too. From what I've seen, anything's possible here." He looked out the window and sighed. "Sadly, I can't stay and help brainstorm. Mal sent me out to find a Road that we supposedly have a traveler on."

"Supposedly?" Molly asked.

"Yeah, the Road coordinates he gave us point to a Road that vanished ten years ago, and the computer can't get a lock on it."

"Fun." Now Molly knew why he'd been out walking in the icy weather. Drew was one of the Gate technicians for Carter's Cove, someone who could feel the magical energy given off by the Roads that crisscrossed the town. Travelers used the Roads to travel between Gates that connected various realms, but every so often a Road would change its course, and wouldn't be able to be connected to a Gate until the coordinates were updated. So the technicians would be sent out to find it, and report back to the engineers, who would reprogram the route, and Mal, the Station manager, who would update the maps.

She also looked out the window and shivered a little. "Would you like something hot to take with you? It's tea, not coffee, but it will keep you warm. Or I could make you hot chocolate."

"Tea would be wonderful. You're my savior." Drew gave her a friendly hug. "I wouldn't say no to a cookie or two either. Just to keep my strength up."

"And what makes you think I have cookies here?" Molly teased him. He was remarkably easy to tease.

"The day Molly Barrett doesn't have cookies in her kitchen is the day the apocalypse starts, or so I've been told," Drew told her.

Molly laughed, unable to deny the truth of that. "Let me see what I can scrape together."

After Drew had left, laden with a travel mug of hot peppermint tea and two cranberry scones in his pocket, Molly sat down at the dining room table and looked at the glittery snow confetti on the floor. Schrodinger had rolled in it, and now silvery snowflakes sparkled in his grey fur as he lay on the window sill.

Drew is a nice guy, she thought, sipping a mug of tea.

He likes you. The CrossCat's thought was sleepy.

"I like him too," she said out loud, reaching out to stroke his soft head. "He seems like a good guy. Maybe we'll get a chance to get to know him better in the next couple of weeks."

That would be good. I like him too, and I think he'd be good for you.

"Do you?" Molly laughed a little. "I'm going to start calling you Yenta, you know."

What's a yenta?

"A matchmaker," she told him.

Because I think he'd be a good friend?

"Is that all you think?"

I don't know yet, Schrodinger said. *But he would be a good friend.*

That Molly couldn't disagree with.

Drew stepped back out into the cold, the travel mug warming his left hand and the tablet back in his right hand. He turned and looked up at the lit window to Molly's apartment, a smile playing over his lips. The warmth of her kitchen had settled around him, and not even the bite of the wind as it followed him down the street could dispel it. The others had been right, damn them. This was a special place.

He hadn't meant this assignment to last more than the year he was required to stay. Carter's Cove was not the big Gate Station that he wanted to manage, but it was a good first step. Or so he'd thought.

And then he'd gotten here, and rather than the cold New England town he'd been warned about, he'd found a home. Now, barely two months after he'd arrived, Drew found himself wondering how hard it would be to extend his contract.

Have to ask Mal about that, he reminded himself. And that thought brought him back to why he was out in the weather. Once again, Drew spread out his senses to the world around him, blocking out the weather as he felt for the magical signature of the Road.

And as he walked down the street, he started to whistle "White Christmas."

The Christmas Can-Can
Friday, December 3

"And how are you doing today, Mrs. Dorr?"

Molly stopped by one of the tables in the tea room to smile down at one of her regular patrons. Mrs. Lucille Dorr was usually accompanied by her husband Stephen, but on Fridays, he met with his book club upstairs, so she would come down with her latest book, her latest project, and drink tea until he was ready to go. Molly enjoyed talking to both of them – they were widely traveled, both mundanely and on the Roads, and they always treated everyone they met as equals who had something fascinating to share.

"I'm good," Mrs. Dorr said, putting an elegant paper lace bookmark in her spot and setting the large book down next to her sage-colored tea cup. Molly had combed through every second-hand store and Goodwill in the fifty miles surrounding Carter's Cove to put together the eclectic tea cup, saucer, and tea pot collection she used in the bookstore. Every piece was different. And if one broke, well, there was always another one in the box she kept in the kitchen. "How are you and Schrodinger doing?" she asked, picking up the knitting in her lap.

"He's obsessed with Christmas and Santa Claus," Molly said,

laughing. "He's never celebrated Christmas, so this is all new to him. It's like living with a six-year-old genius. I never know what he's going to do or say next."

"Makes life interesting," Mrs. Dorr said, nodding her head. "We've met a few on our travels, but were never lucky enough to have one wish to stay with us for long. You're a very lucky girl to have him want to live with you."

"Oh yes, I know." Molly looked over to where Schrodinger was curled up in his bed by the wood stove. His head was resting on the lap of Sarah, Jamie's daughter, who was running her fingers over the pages of a book, her lips moving. Over the quiet rumble of the store, Molly couldn't hear what she was saying, but she bet the child was reading to the CrossCat. "He's so much fun, though. I can't believe it's only been eight months since he came here. I can't imagine life without him now."

"I don't think any of us can," Mrs. Dorr said. "And he's practical, too. Which will be good, because you can't stay single forever." She smiled as Molly wrinkled her nose. "You can't, my dear. Speaking of which, I hear Tom Alward is back in town."

Molly blinked, surprised. "Is he? I though he was gone for a year assignment! It's only been a few months!"

Mrs. Dorr picked up her tea cup, a knowing twinkle in her eyes. "Katarina down at the overnight cafe said he came in Monday night, really late. Looking exhausted, according to her, but happy to be home."

"Anyone who's grown up in the Cove is happy to come home," said a deep voice from behind her, and Molly turned to see Tom himself there. "I think it might be genetic."

Emotions welled up as she looked at the tall, dark-haired tech that she'd once thought she'd marry: joy at seeing him again, worry at how thin he was, and, down beneath, still the anger that he'd ignited with his secrets. But the joy won out, at least for the moment, and she put the tea carafe down and threw her arms around him. "I think you may be right. It's so good to see you again!"

"Is it?" he said, a teasing note in her voice, but she heard the question underneath it.

"Of course it is," she said, squeezing him again. "You know I'll always welcome you back. That's what friends do."

He rested his cheek on her dark hair. "I'm glad we're still friends, Molldoll."

The endearment caused a bit of a flutter in her stomach. The name itself dated back to when she, Tom, and the rest of their small gang decided at the age of eight to become superheroes. Tom had resurrected the name when they'd started dating, and after August, she'd pretty much resigned herself to never hearing it again. She wasn't sure she wanted to, but at the same time, she had missed it.

"We'll always be friends," she told him now firmly. "Can I get you something?"

He shook his head, and Molly noticed the shadows under his eyes. Still exhausted, she realized, and wondered just what kind of assignment he'd taken. Mal hadn't been willing to talk about it, but that wasn't surprising – the Station Manager didn't like to discuss station business with anyone who didn't need to know. And she fell into that category now. *I gave up the right to know where he was going when I threw him out. At least it looks like we'll still be friends.*

Are you okay? Schrodinger asked her, and she looked over her shoulder. The CrossCat hadn't moved, but she saw his tail twitching.

I'm fine, she said firmly. *Enjoy your story.*

"Well, then, give me a moment to check on everyone else, and then we can catch up in the kitchen, before you fall over," she said out loud, turning back to Tom.

The tables were all full, as usual; Molly made a quick circuit around the room, making sure everyone was all set and then she went back into the kitchen. Tom had already gone in and hung his coat up on one of the hooks, as he'd always done, and snagged a stool.

"So, tell me what you can, while I get some food and tea into you," she said, pulling out a mug. "What would you like?"

"Darjeeling, if you have it handy."

Molly rolled her eyes melodramatically. "This is a TEA shop," she reminded him. "I think I might have some Darjeeling lying around." She went into the small pantry and emerged a few minutes later with a silver tea ball that she dropped into the mug. Then she poured boiling water from the kettle on the stove and brought the mug over to Tom. As she handed him the mug, she noticed how very pale his skin was. As if he hadn't seen the sun in months. "So, what brings you home early? I thought Mal said you were supposed to be gone for almost a year?"

Tom took the chain of the tea ball and started to play with it, not looking at her directly. "We were supposed to be there a year," he admitted. "Things got...difficult. That's about all I can tell you. Oh, and it was cold as hell there."

"Colder than here?" she teased lightly, trying to cheer him up.

"Much." He shivered, even in the warm kitchen, and Molly saw a cloud of darkness pass over his blue eyes. "I wasn't sure I'd ever get warm again."

"And how long are you home?" she asked him, laying a hand on his. His fingers squeezed hers once in thanks.

"I don't know. At least through New Year's, barring any emergencies that need a Gate tech," he said. "With the new guy Drew here, we're actually at full strength now. I think Mal might want to keep it that way for as long as he can, especially over Christmas." He sipped his tea and looked at her. "What are you baking today?"

"I don't know yet," Molly admitted, wandering back into the pantry. They didn't really NEED anything, but she always thought better when she was making something, and now was as good a time as any to start for tomorrow.

She came back out with flour and sugar, the basic building blocks, then pulled a brick of cold unsalted butter from the fridge. She bit her lip thoughtfully as she surveyed the contents of the fridge, then pulled out eggs, some cream and, after a minute, some of her friend Lisa's raspberry jam as well.

"Whatever it is will be amazing," Tom said. "That's one thing I've definitely missed: your cooking. Our cook was barely competent, never mind a kitchen witch."

"You've gotten spoiled, eating here," Molly chided him, starting to cream butter and sugar together. "I'll bet your cook was fine."

"He burnt steak," Tom told her. "And his scrambled eggs would make you scream."

They chatted the way old friends do, without any of the awkwardness she'd been worried about, as she mixed up cookie dough. *Almost like the old times,* she though, placing the dough in the fridge to chill before she rolled it out. *As if the break-up hadn't happened...*

And then Tom asked, "So Moll, any plans for tonight?" A casual question, but she could hear the layers to it.

"Not really," she said, forcing herself to smile as she turned back to him. "Schrodinger and I were going to get a pizza and watch a movie. I'm introducing him to all the Christmas classics."

Tom smiled, but the smile never quite made it to his eyes. Something she'd noticed the last few months of their relationship as well. "Sounds like fun," he said. "Don't worry, I'm not looking for an invite." Then he paused. "Unless you're offering one. I heard you haven't been getting out much recently."

"It's been cold and I've been busy," she replied, a little defensively. Then she sighed. "I'm sorry, Tom. I just..."

"I know," he said. "You don't have to apologize, Molly. It's going to be a bit awkward for a while. I don't want to lose you as a friend, though. You mean too much to me. You always did."

"Not enough to tell me everything."

The words slipped out before Molly could stop them, and she winced at the look of pain that sped across Tom's face.

"I'm sorry," she started, but he shook his head.

"No, I deserved that." Tom sighed, getting up and grabbing his coat. He slipped it on, reaching into his pocket for his gloves, and said, "Oh crap, I almost forgot." He handed her the red envelope that had nearly fallen to the floor. "DC asked me to give this to you as I passed by the checkout counter. She said it had come in the mail earlier."

Molly nodded and slid open the envelope. Another CD, of course, with a parchment that said, "Dear Molly, remember that every day needs a bit of fun in it, no matter what else happens. Enjoy this fun. SA"

"That's something you don't see every day," Tom said, looking curiously at the little disc. "And that's a really flimsy envelope to send it in. You're lucky it didn't snap in half."

"I think they're being hand-delivered," Molly said, opening the CD and walking over to the stereo. "There hasn't been any sort of address on it – just my name. Our postmistress is nice, but I'm pretty sure that she wouldn't accept that sort of anonymous stuff through the system."

"True." Tom listened as the music filled the room. "Wait, them? You've gotten more than one? Who is sending them?"

"Haven't a clue," she told him. "I've gotten one every day this month so far. Each one with a CD and a note signed SA. Drew was there when I found yesterday's."

"One a day," Tom said, grinning, but she noticed the smile didn't get all the way to his eyes again. "A nifty Advent calendar, from a secret admirer. You should enjoy it."

"I am," Molly admitted. "And Schrodinger is too."

Schrodinger is too what? The CrossCat sauntered in, his tail swishing behind him.

"Enjoying the cards from SA," Molly said, as Schrodinger jumped up onto his customary stool and looked over at Tom. "Tom brought in today's card."

Oh? That distracted Schrodinger. *What did the note say?*

Molly read it out to him, and when she looked up, Tom had gone. She sighed, and Schrodinger looked over at her.

Are you okay? Was he mean to you?

The fierceness in the CrossCat's voice made her smile. "He wasn't mean," she assured him. "Quite the opposite."

I thought he was supposed to be gone for a year.

"Me too, but he said the assignment changed." Molly sighed. "That's it. As usual."

Schrodinger leaned up against her, a purr rumbling through him. *You can't change him, Molly. He's got to want to tell you.*

"I know." She stroked the side of his head. "I know."

They sat and listened to the CD play "The Christmas Can-Can," and in spite of her worries about Tom, Molly realized that she hadn't lied to him. She WAS enjoying having these little messages sent to her. It was fun. And light-hearted.

I just wish we knew who SA was, Schrodinger said.

"What, you don't think it's Santa anymore?" Molly said, putting the card aside and going to get his tea mug.

I don't know, Schrodinger confessed. *Who else could it be?*

"I don't know either," Molly said, but she wondered.

<><>

Tom hunched his shoulders in his coat as he walked out, giving DC a quick nod. The thought that he was running away from Molly, again, pushed him out the door and into the cool December air. *I do have to get back to the Station, though,* he told himself. *I need to see what Mal has for the schedule.*

Liar, the little voice in his head jeered. *You know exactly what the schedule is – Mal emailed it to you. It hasn't changed since you checked it this morning. You're going in to talk to Drew and Luke. Admit it, at least to yourself. You want to find out what they know about this SA sending messages to Molly. And you know that the Trio won't talk to you about it.*

He climbed into his car and sighed. That, at least, maybe would change now. Molly's three best friends had been unanimous in their support of her, and when she'd thrown him out, had quickly presented a united closed front. His questions and phone calls had gone unanswered. Not that he'd expected anything different, but still…

Throwing the Mercedes into gear, Tom backed out of his spot and headed out to the Gate Station. He still needed to clean up his room there anyways – his mother had been pleased to have him back at the house, but he was feeling the need to get away. As long as he had the option, that was.

He stuck his head into Mal's office when he got to the Station, and received the affirmative. The upper floor of the Gate Station was rooms for all the techs, engineers, and any travelers that might need a bed for a few hours. Even with the new guy, his room was still available.

And covered with dust, Tom found, as he opened his door and sneezed. "We left it just like you asked," he muttered to himself. "I didn't mean that literally, you know, guys."

"Mean what?"

Tom turned quickly to see the new guy coming out of the room across the hall. "Hey, Drew," he said, forcing a friendly smile on his face. "Settling in?"

"For the most part," Drew said, nodding. "Carter's Cove is a great place."

"Yes," Tom said, forcing down his emotions. "Hey, I heard Molly Barrett is getting some Christmas carols from a secret admirer."

Drew went still for just a moment, but Tom noticed the flicker of something behind his eyes. "Did she get one today?" Drew asked innocently.

Not buying it, not for a moment. "Yes, she did," Tom said. "Know anything about it?"

"Only that she's been getting them," Drew said. "What did she get today?"

"The Christmas Can-Can."

A half-smile tugged at Drew's mouth. "I like that song," he said, and then, before Tom could say anything else, Drew closed his door. "I've got to head on to shift. Good luck cleaning up your room."

"Thanks." Tom watched the other man head down the hall. "Thanks."

God Rest Ye Merry, Gentlemen
Saturday, December 4

The bookstore had closed an hour ago. Aunt Margie had departed soon afterward, telling Molly not to stay too late. "Don't forget, Father Christopher is bringing the choir in tomorrow," she'd said, pausing on the doorstep. Behind her, Molly could see her Uncle Art in the car, waiting patiently for his wife. "Do you have everything you need done?"

"That's why Schrodinger and I are staying late," Molly had said, grinning and waving to her uncle, who had looked at his watch pointedly. "The girls are coming over to help us finish up. Go to your dinner date."

Aunt Margie had winked at her. "And if the Terrible Trio can't help you figure out who your secret admirer is, no one can." She'd then sailed down the steps, pleased to have had the last word.

Molly had laughed, but she didn't bother trying to deny it.

The Terrible Trio, aka Sue Elder, Noemi Miller and Lai Zhao, were Molly's best friends in the world, besides Schrodinger. And now, considering that Tom was home, and everything else, she'd decided that she needed them more than ever.

They'd been inseparable until college, when they'd spread out across the United States. But they'd all come back to the Cove, and picked up where they'd left off. They'd also joined ranks with her when she'd thrown Tom out, and she needed to tell them that it was okay. They were a bit…protective of her, to say the least.

They love you, Schrodinger said.

"They do," Molly agreed. "And really, I don't mind. But Tom and I are okay again, and they need to know that."

Schrodinger contented himself with a sniff, and Molly chuckled.

Then, precisely on time, the doorbell rang. Schrodinger jumped down from the stool where he'd been sitting watching Molly cut out sugar cookies, and ran out to the front of the store to open the door, shouting mentally, *Merry Christmas! We have so much to tell you!*

"I can only imagine!" Sue was the first through the front door as he pushed it open and danced back. She shook wind-blown snow from her short ash-blonde hair and grinned at him. Behind her were Noemi and Lai, each of them carrying a large bag similar to Sue's. "Where does Molly want us to set up?"

"Come on back into the kitchen," Molly called out, picking up the last tray of cookies and sliding them into the oven, then cleaning off the island hastily. "And Schrodinger, please lock the front – we're not expecting anyone else."

Will do! Two large paws landed on the door, pushing it closed, and then he went over to the alarm system and jumped up, one claw hitting precisely the center of the button to enable the alarm. Then he trotted back into the kitchen.

"So, put us to work," Sue said, once they'd settled onto stools and Molly had set out, not mugs, but wineglasses. Lai pulled a bottle of red wine from her bag and filled the glasses. "You said you needed help decorating."

"I do, but not just with the cookies." Molly had been thinking about this conversation all afternoon. "I don't know if you've heard, but there's something weird going on, and I need some help figuring this out."

"Ooh, a mystery!" Noemi's blue eyes twinkled mischievously from behind her wire-rimmed glasses. "Does it have to do with a certain Gate Tech whose name we do not speak about coming home early from his assignment?"

Lai scowled. "I hope it doesn't," she said, twining a lock of her long dark hair around one of her elegantly-manicured fingers. "He shouldn't have come back."

"HE has actually already stopped by, and we're okay," Molly told her. "I don't think he had anything to do with these notes, though. He looked really surprised when I told him I'd gotten more than one, and he's not that good an actor."

Lai snorted, and Schrodinger echoed her snort.

"So he really did stop in," Sue said. "I'd heard that." When Molly looked over at her, she shrugged. "We worry. And people talk. Welcome to living in a small town."

"Well, we're good," Molly said firmly. "We're friends. That's it."

"Okay, so what else?" Noemi asked. "If you aren't asking us to defend your honor, what do you need help with?" Her eyes twinkled again. "Christmas cards from a certain SA?"

How did you know? Schrodinger demanded, as Molly went into the pantry and pulled out the small basket.

"I heard it at the post office," Noemi admitted. "Laura the postmistress was telling everyone that she has no idea who was sending them to you, but that they weren't coming through her."

"I figured," Molly said, picking up her wineglass as the others looked at the little envelopes. "They have to be hand-delivered – I just wish I could figure out who was delivering me mini CDs."

"Mini CDs? Seriously?" Noemi pulled one of the envelopes out of the basket and looked at it.

"Seriously," Molly said. "They all have Christmas carols on them. And they must be from the same person or persons – they all have a note with gorgeous calligraphy on it. And they started showing up on December 1."

"The same day Tom came back to the Cove," Sue said, looking at one of the scraps of paper. "You're right, this is gorgeous. Can Tom do calligraphy?"

"I have no idea," Molly said. "I've never seen him do it, but that means nothing." It still stung a bit to say that, but she stuffed that thought back down. "But it's starting to weird me out a little, and you guys are the only ones I can trust not to laugh at me. Or pat me on the head and tell me to just enjoy it, it's romantic."

"Well, it could be romantic, if you had an idea of who it was," Lai said. "Can you put them in order? Maybe we can find a pattern in the songs or something." She picked up one of the CD cases and inspected it. "They aren't marked or anything, are they?"

"No, nothing on the cases, except the name of the song, which I wrote on there so I'd remember." Molly took the CD case back from her, then laid out the cases and the scraps of parchment together in order. "December 1, We Need a Little Christmas. December 2, Let It Snow. December 3, The Christmas Can-Can."

"I love that song!" Sue said, giggling. "At least he has good taste, whoever he is."

Molly laughed in spite of her worries. "He does, doesn't he? I just wish I knew who he was, so I could tell him so."

"And what did you get today?" Noemi asked.

"God Rest Ye Merry, Gentlemen." Molly pointed to the last pile.

Noemi picked up the scrap of paper next to the mini CD and read it out loud. "Dear Molly, sometimes you need friends around you. You seem so lonely all the time, even when you smile. Do something fun with friends tonight. SA."

"Wow, whoever he is, he does seem to know you," Lai said. "Although again, it's not really news that you don't go out much, except the occasional Saturday night when we can drag you out."

"I'm busy most nights," Molly replied a little tartly, getting up and pulling out the last batch of cookies from the oven. "Do you guys think the cookies and the goodies here bake themselves? Never mind the fact that I get up very early most mornings."

That would be really cool if they baked themselves, Schrodinger said, his eyes wide with wonder. *Do you think you could really do that as a kitchen witch, Molly?*

The question made her laugh, and chased away her annoyance. "I don't know," she admitted. "I've never tried it before."

If you do, we should wait for Lily and Jack, he said. *They would be mad if they missed it.*

"Heck, you'd better wait for me, I'd be mad if I missed it too!" Lai said, and the other two agreed.

"I'll let you all know," Molly said, giggling a little. "Now, back to the business at hand."

"Decorating cookies," Sue agreed, reaching into her back and pulling out the decorating kit she'd brought with her. "This will work, right? We found them at that pastry store you like in Portland."

"They're perfect!" Molly said, as Lai and Noemi followed suit. She took the last tray of cooling cookies into the pantry, along with the basket of CDs that Noemi had picked up for her, then came back out with another tray of cookies, these ones glowing with a coat of silvery-white glaze.

"So I'm assuming you don't want us to beat up Tom," Sue said, reaching for a cookie and eying the choices in the decorating kit.

"I'd really rather you didn't, no," Molly told her, rolling her eyes a little bit. "Not until he deserves it, anyways."

Lai muttered something under her breath, but shook her head when the others looked at her, and took a cookie as well.

"So what do you want us to do?" Sue continued. "Find out who's trying to romance you?"

"Trying to romance me?" Molly scoffed. "Hardly."

"That attitude might be why they're trying the subtle way, you know," Noemi said, opening the decorating kit and selecting a tube of silvery snowflakes. "Everyone knows what happened in August, and this person may just want to show you that there's some romance left in the world."

"Maybe." Molly went to the fridge and pulled out a few pastry bags, already filled with red, green, and blue colored icing. Warming them in her hands, she set them on the island, keeping a red one for herself. "But I think I'd be happier if this mystery person just came out and told me, you know? I hate games like this."

"Well, if it IS Tom, I can see why he wouldn't," Lai said, taking a bag of green icing. She frowned at the kit in front of her and continued, "After all, he knows that he screwed up. I'm surprised Aunt Margie let him back in here, to be honest."

He came in while she wasn't here, Schrodinger said helpfully. *And was gone before she came back. But she wasn't happy about it.*

"Thanks," Molly said wryly. "But Aunt Margie now knows that he and I have patched things up." She sighed. "I hated being that angry at him."

"He deserved it." Noemi said flatly, and the other two agreed.

"Did he?" Molly shrugged. "We both behaved badly." Really badly. The last fight had been horrific, truth be told. Both of them screaming at each other, Molly crying and accusing him of cheating, Tom vehemently denying it but refusing to tell her where he'd been, and then, at the end, at least one box of something (she couldn't honestly remember what now – books, maybe?) being thrown out her open window to the alley below. That lovely episode was followed by a three-day withdrawal on her part to her bedroom, where she held on to Schrodinger and cried. A lot. By the time she'd come out, Tom had gone, headed out to the assignment that was going to take him away for a year, and she'd decided it was for the best.

"Anyways, I really don't think it's him," she said, shaking her head. "He's just not that good an actor."

"Maybe." Noemi sounded doubtful. "We never thought he'd break your heart, either. Everyone changes."

"But he's not the only candidate in town, you know," Sue said, and they all looked at her. "Oh, come on. Really, Molly?"

"Who?" Molly demanded, confused.

"Well, neither Drew nor Luke have girlfriends," Lai said pointedly.

"They're both busy too," Molly said. "And I've known Luke forever. He thinks of me as a sister, not as a girlfriend."

"Funny, I believe I remember her saying the very same thing

about Tom, don't you?" Sue said, turning to Noemi and Lai, who both nodded.

"And just because they don't have girlfriends--" Molly said.

"And tend to stop in here a lot," Sue interjected blandly, and Molly scowled at her.

"Lots of people stop in here a lot. It's a bookstore, remember? And this is rural Maine – it's not like there's a lot to do here in the Cove in the winter." Molly felt herself starting to blush as they continued to grin at her. "Maybe they just like to read. Or they like to drink tea. Lots of people drink tea."

"Uh-huh." Lai, Noemi, and Sue all shared another knowing glance before Lai continued, "And it just so happens that some of the Cove's most eligible young bachelors all have cravings for tea and books lately."

Molly tried to glare at all of them but gave up. "All right, fine," she said, a smile pulling at her lips. "I doubt it's Luke, though – he barely says three words to me, and he buys books, not tea." She arched an eyebrow at Sue. "And I hear he's been by the museum an awful lot lately too."

Sue blushed, but shot back, "He's lulling you into a false sense of security."

"Do you mind?" Molly said, chuckling. "I'll give you Drew, though. I can't seem to turn around lately without tripping over him."

"Not that you mind," Lai said. "I hear you sent him out with tea the other day."

"It was cold out," Molly said. "I was being nice."

"What about the new elementary school principal?" Noemi said. "He's been here an awful lot. What's his name – Matt?"

"Mark," Molly corrected her automatically, and they all laughed. "All right, fine, maybe him too. Although really, he's flirted more with DC than he has with me."

"Well, you can't have them all," Sue teased her. "But he is cute. And single."

And so they talked on, discussing and discarding potential suspects as they decorated plate after plate of cookies that Molly had baked that afternoon. And later, when they all finally left, all three promised to keep their eyes open.

"After all, we can't have you being too creeped out to go out with us," Sue said. "It's hard enough to convince you to come!"

I'll protect her, Schrodinger promised.

"We know you will," Lai assured him. "And when we figure out who it is…" She didn't finish the sentence, but nodded mock-menacingly. All four of them burst into laughter.

Molly just hoped they'd all be laughing when they figured it out.

Carol of the Bells
Sunday, December 5

Molly sank down into one of the easy chairs that had been pushed into a corner of the large upstairs room of the CrossWinds Bookstore and let the music wash over her. Father Christopher had arranged with Aunt Margie to bring the Carter's Cove Christmas Choir over to serenade the store, as he done every year since he'd come to the Cove. The achingly beautiful music filled every inch of the building; and Molly loved to listen.

The choir stood with their backs to the great stone fireplace that dominated one end of the room, the gold and green of their robes brilliant against the dark wood and stone of the hearth. Aunt Margie had hung stockings along the mantel for all the staff, as she had done every year, and Schrodinger had been thrilled to see a red and white velveteen stocking with his name among them. The hearth was bracketed by two full evergreen Christmas trees that sparkled with thousands of tiny white lights. The decorations hadn't changed in Molly's memory: the entire store was always decorated with snowflakes, candy canes, and other decorations that spoke of New England Christmases of old. Molly decided, once again, that it was perfect. Atop each tree, a white star sparkled, crocheted by Mrs.

Dorr, and that too was perfect.

Schrodinger climbed up into her lap, just like a regular tabby cat but larger, and purred a deep mellow harmony over which the clear voices of the choir floated. Molly stroked his silky fur gently as she watched the singers. Once again, Father Christopher had brought together not just the parishioners of the Cove's Catholic Church, but anyone from the surrounding community and Realms who wanted to sing. The chorus this year included: two sea elves, their beautiful pale skin slightly iridescent, reflecting the Christmas lights; a Kadar who had just happened to come into town as the season was starting and decided to stay long enough to sing, his long dark beard nearly brushing the floor as it wiggled in time to the music; two harpists from the Darjeeling Road that came every year to perform with the choir; and, much to everyone's surprise, one of the reclusive Mareesh, a dark-skinned young woman with ebony stars in her eyes instead of irises, and intricate white tattoos covering her face and hands. This was in addition to the normal church choir, which boasted a centaur with an amazing baritone, among others.

You know, I think that's one of the best parts of living in the Cove, Molly thought, still stroking Schrodinger and letting the music flow through her. The entire bookstore had stopped in their tracks to listen. *You never know who you're going to run into.*

Agreed, Schrodinger said sleepily, his head resting on his paws. *And even if there's a portion that's nasty, most are not.*

No, most aren't, Molly agreed. *And everyone has your back.*

That's because it's a small town. Small towns are like family.

The final notes of the last carol hung in the air like shimmering snowflakes, and then everyone burst into applause. After the clapping ended, most of the singers and the audience moved to the tables Aunt Margie and DC had set up the night before on the right side of the room, where all the cookies Molly and the Trio had decorated were waiting for them, along with veggie trays, tea sandwiches, and other assorted goodies for all species present. There were two large crock pots of mulled cider, and one of mulled wine (which DC was standing behind, watching like a hawk) and bottled water. And a large hot water carafe as well, for tea, of course.

"Once again, my dear Molly, you have outdone yourself."

Molly looked up and saw Father Christopher himself smiling down at her, carrying a plate filled with goodies. The good priest was in his sixties, but seemed to have changed little in the fifteen years since he'd come to the Cove. She wondered, not for the first time, what he'd thought when he'd looked out on his congregation that first Sunday. Father Christopher had grown up and had his first few parishes in the San Francisco area. *Then again, even though it's not a CrossRoads town, we are talking about San Francisco,* she thought. *Really, there's probably nothing here in the Cove that can hold a candle to there on any given day, Gate or no Gate.*

And it's warmer there, Schrodinger added sleepily, and Molly chuckled.

What does that have to do with anything? She asked.

Things are always weirder the warmer it gets. Less layers to hide the weirdness.

Molly couldn't argue with that. "Thank you," she said out loud, smiling up at the silver-haired priest. "You did too. The music was lovely."

"We had a very good choir this year," he agreed, settling in to the easy chair next to her. "Starsha in particular was amazing. That was a real feather in the church's cap, and I hope she stays."

"Starsha?" Molly asked.

Father Christopher nodded at the young Mareesh as she stood talking to Pertwee, the centaur, her hands tucked into the sleeves of her choir robe. "She has a voice like an angel, as you heard. And it took a lot for her to convince her parents, her father in particular, to let her come to the Cove to participate, but she did it. I don't know how. She's actually hoping to stay and take voice lessons from Darian."

"Wow, really?" Molly looked over at Starsha with a new appreciation. "Do you think she'll be able to convince him to take her as a student?" The Minstrel had retired to the Cove a few years earlier, and she knew he'd already turned away a few prospective students that hadn't met his high standards. It took a lot to be a Minstrel, one of the traveling musicians who wandered the Roads, and Darian had always said he would not waste his time training someone who wouldn't be able to handle the rigors of the job.

"I think so, yes. She's determined to be a Minstrel," Father Christopher said. "And she's got the chops to do it. Don't let her appearance fool you – that girl is made of steel covered in silk. And it would be criminal for that voice not to be heard."

Molly couldn't argue with that. "So has she approached him?"

Father Christopher nodded. "They met at the church a few weeks ago, and he's been stopping in to listen to the choir. I think today was the last part of her audition," he said, pointed with a tea sandwich across the room, where a tall, slender elf in jeans and a faded flannel shirt was talking to Aunt Margie, his long silver braid down over one shoulder. "Because Darian doesn't usually come to this."

"No, he doesn't." The Minstrel didn't come in to the Cove very much at all – he was a homebody, but about once every two months, Darian came to the bookstore for more reading material and a supply of the special tea that Molly ordered for him. He'd made his supply run the week before Thanksgiving, as usual, since he didn't like to deal with the tourists who flocked to the Cove during the Christmas season. "Do you think he'll take her?"

"After that performance? I'd be surprised if he didn't. He was just waiting to see how she handled crowds, and she was flawless." Father Christopher finished his sandwich and put the plate down on the table between them, then leaned in towards her and said softly, "I have something for you. It was left at the church this morning."

Molly raised an eyebrow at him, and then felt her heart flutter as he pulled a familiar red envelope out of his shirt pocket. He handed it to her, and she felt the CD case inside, along with something else – something hard and bulky. "Left at the church, you say."

He nodded, but there was a twinkle in his blue eyes. Molly suspected he knew more about this whole thing than he was admitting, but knew better than to ask. Father Christopher took the whole priest-parishioner privilege very seriously. "I heard a rumor that this isn't the first red envelope you've received," he said, sitting back in his chair and watching her intently.

"News travels fast in the Cove," Molly said, opening the envelope over Schrodinger's back as the CrossCat, now completely awake, twisted to try and see what she was doing. As always, the mini CD slid out, but accompanying it this time was a silver jingle bell that chimed as it rolled into her hand. "Apparently I'm being courted. Or something."

"Or something?" Father Christopher echoed, chuckling a little. "You sound uncertain. Being courted isn't a bad thing, last time I checked."

"Not usually, but it can be when you don't know who's courting you," Molly replied, uncurling the scrap of parchment from where it was tied to the bell. "Then it's kind of creepy, actually."

"Don't you have any ideas?" the priest asked, watching her read the note.

"No," Molly said. "I don't know anyone with the initials SA, after all, and that's how they've all been signed. And if it is a secret admirer, the way Aunt Margie thinks, then I'm still at a loss. Who would send these things and not want me to know who it is?"

"And there aren't clues in the notes?" Father Christopher asked.

"If there are, I'm not smart enough to decipher them," Molly said, letting some of the frustration she felt leak into her tone. "Look for yourself." She handed the bell over to him.

Father Christopher looked at the scrap, which read, "In the darkest night, when all hope is lost, listen to this and remember that I'm still here for you. SA" He blinked. "Well, that's a nice sentiment, but cryptic."

"Very," Molly agreed.

I think it's Santa, Schrodinger said, turning his head to look at the priest. *I've asked for a special present, and I think this is his way of telling me he's working on it.*

"If that's the case, then why are the cards coming to Molly, instead of you?" Father Christopher asked.

Because the present is for Molly, not for me, Schrodinger said, and Molly hoped that would be the end of it. She'd explained to the Cross Cat that not everyone needed to know what his wish was for, and when he'd expressed confusion about that, had fallen back on the idea that if he told everyone his wish, it might get lost in the background noise that Santa heard around Christmas every year. That had convinced him for the moment, but she wasn't sure how long it would last, especially if people kept asking him.

Father Christopher, however, simply nodded. "So the notes let you he's gotten your message, and that he's working on it. I can see that." He stroked Schrodinger's head. "I hope it comes true for you."

It will, Schrodinger said. *I have faith.*

"We should all have faith," Father Christopher agreed, and got up. "Thank you again, Molly."

Christmas Wrapping
Monday, December 6

"**H**ey, Molly, you busy?"

Noemi stuck her head around the doorway to the kitchen, her bright blue eyes twinkling, then she blinked when she didn't get an answer. Molly was bent over the oven, carefully pulling out trays of cookies one at a time and setting them on the counter beside the oven. There was a steady stream of low curses coming from her direction, and Noemi doubted Molly had even heard her come in. The smell of burnt cookies hung in the air.

Something tapped at her leg. Noemi looked down and saw Schrodinger standing beside her.

Can I help? Molly's not really in a good mood right now, he said. *I wouldn't go in there.*

Giving the situation another look, Noemi realized he was probably right. They both backed carefully out of the kitchen doorway and into the warm tea room.

Instead of settling in his bed beside the wood stove in the tea room, Schrodinger led her out to the front room, and leaped into her lap once she settled into one of the armchairs scattered about the bookstore. Noemi stroked his soft head and asked, "What's wrong with Molly?

She never burns cookies."

She's having a bad day. Schrodinger leaned into the caress. *And she doesn't like not knowing who SA is, or having folks laugh off her concerns about it.*

Noemi could appreciate that. "Do you know who he is, Schrodinger?" she asked, scratching him under the chin. "You'd tell her if you knew, right?"

Of course I would! He pulled back from her, an offended look in his eyes. *Why would I keep that from her?*

"Sorry," Noemi said soothingly. "I know you would." She sighed, and stroked his head again. After a moment, he leaned back against her, accepting the apology. "So what happened today to give her a bad day?"

Tom came in earlier. I was asleep in the tea room when he came in, but she shouted something at him and he stomped out, which woke me up. The purr in his throat died, and he made an unhappy sound. *She wouldn't even tell me what was wrong – she just started making cookies and burning them. So I've stayed out of her way.*

"Good idea." Noemi winced and wondered what Tom had said to her.

I hope Tom isn't her secret admirer, Schrodinger said softly, laying his head against her chest. *Is that bad?*

"No." Noemi didn't mention that most of Molly's friends hoped Tom wasn't her secret admirer, although the information she'd come to share with Molly seemed to point towards his involvement. The break-up between the two of them had done some serious damage to Molly and her confidence, and even though Molly had said she and Tom were okay, they obviously weren't.

Noemi herself was hoping it was gentle, quiet Luke who was behind the notes: he was content to remain in the background most of the time, as he had during most of their childhood, but he was fiercely loyal, and he knew how to treat a lady. And that, as her grandmother liked to remind her, was important.

Now, she said, "No, it's not bad. It means you love her, and realize that he's not going to make her happy in the end." *I just hope he realizes it soon.*

They were still sitting there when Aunt Margie came through. The woman stopped, startled. "Noemi! What are you doing out here?"

"Thinking of how to beard Molly in her den without losing fingers," Noemi said, and then saw the red envelope in Aunt Margie's hand. "Oh no, not another one."

"Yes." Aunt Margie looked amused, not worried, and breezed by them into the kitchen. Schrodinger and Noemi exchanged looks, then followed in her wake.

"I'm a bit busy now, and not in the mood for company." Molly's voice was curt, full of barely-repressed rage, quite at odds from the steady hand and delicate butter cream she was frosting the cookies in front of her with. Noemi noticed the scent of burnt cookies had faded, and around the kitchen were trays of cookies in various stages of completion: some raw dough, ready to go into the oven; some cooling on racks, golden brown and fragrant; and some fully covered in frosting and arranged on silver trays. Noemi was a bit awed by the sheer volume of cookies, and wondered if she could filch one without pissing Molly off even more.

"And I'm wondering what happened earlier," Aunt Margie said crisply, crossing her arms over her chest. "I appreciate that you two kept your voices down, but I had four separate patrons tell me you and Tom had words in here. What happened, and do I need to ban him from the store?"

Molly threw her spatula into the bowl of butter cream. "No, you don't need to ban him," she said crossly. "He now knows he's not welcome here right now."

"So what did he do?" Noemi asked timidly, not sure she wanted to know.

"He asked me to the Snow Queen's ball," Molly snapped, and then, when Aunt Margie started to chuckle, glared at her. "This is not funny!"

"He actually asked you out?" Noemi said, eyes wide. "Really?"

Aunt Margie just laughed. "Of course he did."

"Not only that," Molly continued, in a low voice as full of venom as Noemi had ever heard. "He didn't ask. He just came in and asked me what color dress I was wearing for the ball, so that we could coordinate. And did I want to do dinner beforehand?"

"Oh." Aunt Margie swallowed her chuckles, while Noemi goggled at Molly. "I see he hasn't learned much in the last few months. But maybe he's just excited to see you again, Molly."

"*I* haven't gone anywhere," Molly said pointedly, picking up her spatula and starting to frost another set of cookies. "*I* wasn't the one who took the assignment that I couldn't tell my girlfriend about, disappeared for three months, and then showed back up, offered no explanation or apology, and asked her to marry me. And was then shocked and hurt when she flipped out. So I don't see why he would be all that excited – or surprised at my reaction."

"He missed you," Aunt Margie said. "And you missed him, or you wouldn't be so pissed at him." When Molly glared at her, her aunt laid the red envelope on the island. "This came for you today in the mail. Maybe it will put you in a better mood."

She left, and Noemi sighed. "I might as well tell you," she said reluctantly. "And don't hate me for it."

"What?" Molly asked. "What bad news do you have for me?" Then she shook her head. "I'm sorry. You didn't deserve that."

Noemi came around and hugged her. "No, it's okay. I understand." Then she took a deep breath and said, "Tom bought two boxes of Christmas cards the night he got back, which was the 30th of November. With red envelopes. My cousin over at the stationary shop told me when I was in there earlier."

The envelope Aunt Margie had laid on the counter sat there, a silent accusation. Molly pulled herself out of Noemi's arms, put the spatula back into the bowl of frosting more gently than she had before, and moved it to the sideboard. Then she picked up the envelope and opened it, dumping out the CD along with the standard scrap of parchment. She looked at the note, growled something under her breath, and stomped out of the kitchen. Schrodinger, after a look at Noemi, followed her.

Once the kitchen was silent, Noemi picked up the note. It said, "Molly, just like the song says, I've been chasing you for a while. I'm hoping this way, I'll be able to catch you by Christmas Day. That would be the best present ever. SA"

<><>

Tom leaned against the cool stone wall of the Station, trying to stifle the pounding in his head. Molly's last words still echoed in his ears.

"You are not the boss of me!" she'd told him, brandishing the spatula in her hand like a sword. "You do not have the right to presume anything about me, or where I go! You gave that up when you lied to me! Get out!"

He'd gotten, and the truth of her words ate into his stomach lining now. The cold wind off the sea brushed over him, not nearly as painful as the ache in his heart.

"It's a bit chilly to be standing out here," a quiet voice interrupted him. Tom opened his eyes to see Luke Travers, the third Gate tech and one of his oldest friends, leaning against the wall next to him.

"Good thinking weather, though," Tom said, shifting a bit so that Luke could join him in the relative shelter that he'd found.

"And you've got a lot of thinking to do?" Luke said, giving him a sideways look.

Tom chuckled ruefully. "What else is new?"

"I heard you and Molly had a blow up again today."

There was nothing but neutrality in Luke's voice, but Tom felt himself recoil from the unspoken accusation. "Yeah, apparently I'm persona non grata around the tea shop right now," he said, grinding his teeth together. "Because I assumed again."

"You have a bad habit of doing that," Luke observed.

"Tell me something I don't know."

"Molly's not the same person you left in August, and you aren't either."

That wasn't what Tom had expected to hear, and he cocked his head, looking over at Luke. "What do you mean?"

The tall tech shrugged, looking out over the snowy lawns. "You've always played your cards close, Tom, but you might as well be mute now. You don't say anything about anything of meaning, and you just assumed she'd wait for you. Molly's never been like that, but she tried to be, for you. And you threw it away, but you didn't realize it."

"Oh, I realized it," Tom said bitterly, remembering the long nights spent alone, replaying his final conversation with Molly before he'd headed out on his assignment.

"No, you didn't," Luke said. "You still don't."

"What's that supposed to mean?"

Luke turned and looked at him squarely, his green eyes unusually serious. "You went and told Molly you were taking her to the Snow Queen's ball today, didn't you?"

"Yes."

"Without asking her if maybe she'd made other plans."

"She hadn't," Tom protested. "I asked around."

"But you didn't ask HER," Luke said, and then nodded when Tom blinked. "You just assumed that she'd be thrilled to go along with you, because she said she didn't want to lose your friendship. But there's a big difference between asking her, and assuming. You've never really understood that, and now that she's forcing you to, you're fighting it."

"And you know this how?" Tom asked, hearing the harshness in his own voice. The accuracy of Luke's observations hurt.

"Because I've been here, and I see it." Luke shrugged. "I'm not the only one." He pushed himself off the wall and turned to Tom. "We've been friends a long time."

"Yes, we have." *Which is why I'm not punching you at the moment.*

"Let me give you some friendly advice, then." Luke paused until Tom nodded, then continued, "Step back from Molly for a bit.

Friends give other friends space when they need it. Let her reach out to you."

"Do you know how hard that is?" Tom asked him.

"I do," Luke said. "I've been the guy in the back for a long time." He gave Tom a rueful smile. "That's what I get for letting you have the spotlight. But you blew it, and now, you have to deal with those consequences. And that includes backing off. Even if you see others stepping up."

He turned around and walked back towards the Station door, while Tom watched him go.

The Holly and The Ivy
Tuesday, December 7

"Bah, humbug."

Molly looked out the window at the snow-covered yard and tried to figure out why she was still so grumpy. Part of it was Tom, of course – why had she thought it would be any different this time? She said friendship, and he thought everything was back to normal, without him having to explain anything. And there was that damn SA too. Who was he? And why couldn't he just come out and tell her who he was, and that he liked her? Why all the secrets?

A noise made her turn from the window; Schrodinger poked his head around the edge of the kitchen doorway and blinked sleepily at her. *Is it time to get up?*

Even wrapped in crankiness, Molly couldn't help smiling at him. The CrossCat was too damn cute for his own good. "Only if you want to share my tea and my grumpy mood," she said. "It's only about 7 am. You could sleep longer."

Yes, but the bed is now cold, because I'm the only one in it. His mental voice was plaintive as he came into the kitchen. *And it's Tuesday. Why did you get up early on a Tuesday? Do we have to make something special? Or be somewhere?*

"No, I just couldn't sleep." Molly looked back out of the window. It was a day that matched her mood: grey, heavy clouds hung low in the sky, sulking just over the tops of the houses and trees. The snowman they had built in the front yard raised lonely hands to the clouds, as if appealing to someone, anyone, to come and join him. His cap, knit by Molly's mother for her two years ago, had slipped down to one side of his head, giving him a slightly rakish, slightly desperate look.

Schrodinger climbed nimbly up into her lap. Instead of curling up as he normally did, though, he faced her, and put a soft paw on her cheek. *Why do you let Tom do that?*

"Do what?"

Fluster you.

Fluster wasn't quite the word Molly would have used to describe her reaction to Tom's latest antics, but it worked. She sighed and stroked his fuzzy head. "I don't know," she admitted. "If I did know, maybe he wouldn't get to me quite so much."

Is it because you still love him? Schrodinger looked up at her. *Do you want him back?*

Molly swallowed. Part of her did, badly, desperately – wanted to recapture the early days of their relationship, when everything in the world had seemed lit from within by her happiness at being his. But another part of her, the wiser part, reminded her about the absences, the long silences where she had no idea where he was, or when he was coming back. While she knew some of that was part of his job as a Gate tech, there had been too many trips on short notice, and too many that hadn't seemed to correspond with anything that had come through the Station. Even Luke had commented on how often he seemed to be gone.

And then there had been that odd message left on her answering machine, the one that had made Tom go white when she'd played it for him, demanding an answer she'd never gotten – a young woman's voice, asking for Tom with an odd accent. The message that had completely shattered her trust in him when he refused to explain it.

Molly?

Schrodinger's questioning voice snapped her out of the memory, and she blinked at him. "Sorry. Old thoughts." Molly shook her head. "Do I still love him? I do. Not in the way I did, but I'll always love him. But I'm not ready to let him waltz back into our lives yet. Not like that. I just don't trust him anymore, and no relationship survives without trust." Then she focused on the CrossCat. "What about you? Do you want him back here?"

Only if you do, Schrodinger said, leaning up against her, his head on her shoulder. His purr vibrated through her, warming her and chasing away her blue mood, at least for a little bit.

Later that afternoon, though, the gloom settled back in, heavy as the clouds pressing down from above. Molly sat at the dining room table, flipping desultorily through her cookbooks, looking for a good recipe to try at the tea house, hoping the familiar act of baking would raise her mood. Schrodinger had gone off to nap in the living room, so she was alone. Problem was, her creativity and impetus to do anything other than sit and stare out her window was as flat as the sky outside.

Then someone knocked on her door. The sound echoed through the silent apartment; Molly jumped, her heart pounding at the sudden noise. Then she shook herself. *Don't be silly. It's probably just one of the Trio looking in on me.*

To her surprise, however, it was Drew standing on the small landing, a large holly wreath in his hands. "Hey," he said, grinning. Then his grin faded a bit at the look on her face. "I come in peace?" And he held out the wreath.

Molly grinned back at him, unaccountably cheered by his presence. "Thank you, but you didn't need to," she said, accepting the wreath. "Come in for some tea? Schrodinger's asleep, and I'm just hanging out."

"How can I refuse that charming offer?" Drew said, following her into the apartment. He pulled off his jacket and hung it up on one of the hooks by the door. "That's from all of us, by the way."

"All of you?" Molly asked, looking closely at the wreath. It was charmingly simple, twined with red holly berries and green ivy leaves, with a small brown birdhouse set in the bottom right hand corner of the inner circle of the wreath. A dark red cardinal perched up in the opposite corner, looking over at his mate who was peeking out of the house.

"Yeah, me, Luke, Mal, Tom, Heidi and Porter," he said, then flushed. "Well, it was going to be from us. But when I got to the stand to buy it…"

"It was already paid for and waiting for you," Molly finished, plucking the telltale red envelope from where it nestled next to the birdhouse. "So you decided to deliver it?"

He nodded. "That way, I could scope out to see if you had a tree yet, so we could get you that."

"You guys don't have to get me anything," Molly told him. "You know that, right?"

"We want to," Drew said. "We really, really appreciate all the cookies and tea and stuff you send over to the Station. Saves us from eating what we can cook." He shuddered dramatically.

Molly laughed a little at that. "Don't let Heidi hear you say that!" she teased, putting the wreath on the counter. "She's a very good cook!"

"Not as good as you."

"I appreciate the sentiment," Molly said. "Too bad my secret admirer beat you to the punch."

"He's got eyes and ears everywhere – we can't compete," Drew said, watching her open the envelope. Inside was the familiar CD and its note. "What does it say?"

"Dear Molly, I saw you had no wreath on your door, and well, pretty girls should have pretty decorations. Thank you for being a lovely part of the Cove. SA." She looked at the CD. "I wonder what carol he sent me this time?"

"I'll take a wild guess and say The Holly and The Ivy, considering that's what the wreath is made of," Drew said.

Molly shook her head irritably. "Why now? Why, after all this time, is Tom playing these silly games?"

"Do you think that's who it is?" Drew asked her.

"Who else could it be?" Molly said. "Most of the guys here in town grew up with me, and treat me like one of their sisters, after all. And this whole business started when he came back from wherever he'd been this time." She was slightly surprised by the bitterness in her voice.

"Look, Molly, I don't want to give you advice or anything. Heck, I've only been here a few months, so I don't want to pretend that I know what went on between you and Tom." Drew hesitated, and Molly could guess why. She was sure he'd been filled in at the station. "But do me two favors, okay?"

She looked at him warily. "Depends on the favors."

"Don't be too hard on Tom," Drew said. "His heart's in the right place, even if he acts like an idiot when he tries to follow it."

"And the second favor?" Molly asked.

He surprised her then by leaning in and brushing a light kiss on her forehead. "Don't believe that every other guy in the Cove thinks of you as his sister. I can tell you that in at least three cases, you're definitely wrong."

Before she could respond, his phone buzzed loudly. He looked at the message on it, swore, and grabbed his coat off the hook. "Sorry, gotta run. Mal says they need me back at the Station."

"Drew," she said hastily, and he paused on the doorstep. "I don't have a tree yet."

He gave her a grin, and then was gone.

Let It Snow
Wednesday, December 8

"Hey, Molly, Schrodinger, need a lift?"

The words, shouted over the roar of the snowmobile that came to a stop in front of her brownstone, sounded like the song of an angel to Molly. She and Schrodinger had been wondering just how they were going to get to the bookstore that morning; the nor'easter that had settled in the night before was still dumping snow, adding nearly a foot to the already impressive amounts on the sidewalks. Sidewalks which at 6 a.m. still hadn't been cleared, although the plow had come through a few times. Molly, with no car, had been on the verge of going back inside and calling for a cab when the snowmobile had come up.

Now, she watched as Luke removed his helmet and gave her his shy smile. Another one of her childhood friends who had gone to Boston to train and then come back home, like Tom, to the Cove. Really, Drew was the anomaly, but Molly had heard mention that he was an orphan, so maybe that was why he'd chosen a new town, rather than go back to his hometown, wherever that was.

Schrodinger looked up at her, snowflakes caught in his whiskers. *Can we?*

"I don't think we have much of a choice, if we want to get to work," she said, hefting her cooler and grinning. "Do you have room for this too, Luke?"

He nodded and cut the engine so they could talk without shouting. "Once we saw it was still snowing, I volunteered to come and get you. Beat Drew and Tom to it by about two minutes." His grin had a triumphant edge to it.

Molly blushed, hearing Drew's words echoing through her head again. "You guys! You're awesome. Mal's going to hate me, though. Stealing away all his Gate techs, just to help me get to work."

"Nah, Mal doesn't mind. I'm off-duty now anyways." Luke climbed off the machine and waded through the snow over to her. "Let me take that. Besides, if you don't get to the store, who's going to send tea and cookies over to the Station later, when I have to go on shift again? This is pure selfishness, I assure you." He took the cooler and offered her an arm, which she took gladly. "And it means I get to ride through downtown with one of the sexiest ladies in the Cove. Talk about street cred."

"You guys are getting your brains scrambled down at the Gate Station," Molly told him. "First Drew, now you – seriously, guys, I'm just a cook in a tea shop. You should know that." She did NOT mention Tom's name.

Luke stopped short and turned to look at her. "You aren't 'just' anything, Molly," he said, and the seriousness of her tone made her blink. "Don't let anyone tell you that, ever. You've never been 'just' anyone. You're very, very important to the Cove and to me." Then he grinned his shy grin again. "Besides, you're sexy, gorgeous, sweet and the best baker in Maine, if not the United States. There's no 'just' about it."

The words, more than she'd heard Luke string together in the past four months, floored her. "Really?" was all she could manage to squeak out.

"Really." Luke jumped down carefully on to the street, put the cooler down, then turned. He put his hands on her waist and lifted her down to join him. "There will be weeping when you finally let someone steal your heart again."

"I think you're all insane," Molly said, climbing on to the snowmobile and turning to watch as he lashed her cooler to the back of the machine. Schrodinger waited until Luke had settled himself in front of Molly, and then jumped in front of the tech and crouched low on the sheepskin buckled on to the front of the seat. "Don't you guys have anything better to do at the Station than talk about me?"

"Sure, but they're not as interesting." Luke handed her a helmet, then put his arms around the CrossCat. "Hold on tight, now; the roads are slicker than they look. Schrodinger, make sure you're anchored, buddy."

Claws are dug in. This was a good idea.

"Drew's," Luke said, and then there was no more time for speaking as he cranked the machine to life. They sped through the pre-dawn twilight, the snow flying by them, and Molly gloried in the feeling. When Luke pulled up in front of the store, she was almost sorry the ride was over.

"That was awesome," she said, handing him back the helmet after she'd clambered off. "Thank you so much."

"No problem." Luke handed her the cooler, and then stowed the extra helmet. "Say, Molly…"

"Yes?" she asked, when he trailed off.

"I know you and Tom had words, but is it true, you aren't going to the Snow Queen's Ball?"

"I don't know," she said after a few minutes, when the snow falling between them was the only sound on the street. "It's a work night…"

"It's also the day that every business in the Cove closes early, and I know for a fact that Aunt Margie gives you that Sunday off," Luke told her. "Not an excuse."

We're not going to the Snow Queen's Ball? Schrodinger asked her, dismay showing in every line of his body. *But I've heard so much about it! How can we miss it?*

"You can't," Luke told him. "Really."

"We'll see," Molly said. "I'm not sure. But if I do go..."

"If you do, save me a dance?"

She nodded, unable to say anything, and he grinned. "I'll be back later for our cookies. Anything good in that cooler today?"

"Walnut Rum balls," she said, and he licked his lips approvingly. "We just got in some lovely new spice teas, so I thought it would go well."

"Good choice," Luke said. And then he was gone, zooming up the street back towards the Station, leaving her standing amid the falling snowflakes and wondering just what had leeched into the water lately to have all the guys she'd thought she'd known turn into strangers.

I like him, Schrodinger announced, bringing her back from her thoughts. *Can we keep him?*

"And where would we keep him?" she teased the CrossCat. But that didn't stop her from wondering for a moment what a relationship with Luke would be like. Certainly different from her time with Tom. Molly shook herself and turned towards the store. "Besides, he's a grown man. It's up to him..."

Her voice trailed off. There, peeking out from the holly leaves of the wreath on the front door, was another red envelope.

She opened it, after they'd warmed up in the store, a steaming cup of the new tea next to her elbow. This time, the CD came out in a cloud of tiny glittery snowflakes that Schrodinger immediately attacked as they danced around the kitchen. For a few moments, Molly simply sat and laughed as she watched him. Then she looked at the scrap of parchment that had come with the CD.

"You look lovely in the snow," it said simply, and was signed, "SA."

<><>

"Molly and Schrodinger safe at the store?" Drew asked, as Luke came into the Gate Room.

"Yep," Luke said, taking a seat next to him at the main computer terminal and letting the warmth of the room melt away the last of the ice in his bones. It had been a cold ride. "And we're getting walnut rum balls later."

"I don't understand why more people don't want this position," Drew said, shaking his head. "Or how you guys aren't all 800 pounds, given that she's been feeding you all these years."

Luke chuckled. "It's all in the pacing. And really, she's only been back at the Cove for about four years. We haven't had much call for new techs."

Drew looked over at him. "So, any news?"

"She's still considering not going, but I think Schrodinger will convince her otherwise," Luke told him. "And before I left, I saw another red envelope."

"Good. SA is still on the job." Drew's attention was drawn back to the monitor as something beeped. As he began typing something in response to the question that had popped up, Luke studied him. He still didn't know why the man had come to the Cove, instead of going back to the Midwest where he'd grown up, but Drew had fit into the (admittedly) insular Gate Station crew very well. At least, until Tom had come back.

It hadn't been a secret around the Station that both Drew and Luke were attracted to Molly, but Tom had seemed very surprised to find it out when he returned. Tom had always been the leader of their group, and finding that he'd been demoted to last place in the race for her affections had left him more than a little abrasive. Luke wondered idly what Tom would do if Molly ended up with someone else. Especially an outsider.

As if Luke's thoughts had summoned him, Tom came into the Gate room. He wasn't on duty either, but he wandered over to them. "Molly get to work okay?"

Luke nodded. "She and Schrodinger enjoyed the snowmobile ride."

"Do you think she's enjoying the cards?" Drew said casually, and Luke saw Tom's lips tighten.

"I think she's growing to," Luke said finally. "Molly loves a good mystery. I think she's just not used to being the center of anyone's attention, and so it's weirding her out a bit."

Tom's lips tightened even more, but Drew cocked his head, considering. "I can see that," Drew said. "She's a lot like you in that, actually, Luke."

"Me?" Luke blinked. "What do you mean?'

"You're very quiet, and always in the background, but you know almost everything that's going on around you. You hate being the center of anyone's attention," Drew said, and then shoved his chair back. "I need to go see Mal about this latest update. Watch the console for me?"

"Sure."

After he'd left, Tom dropped down into his seat and scowled. "Did you have to do that?"

"Do what?"

"Point out to him how I screwed up."

"Is that what you thought I meant?" Luke shook his head. "Dude, get over it. I just meant that Molly doesn't like putting herself forward."

"Because I didn't make her the center of my universe," Tom said.

"That's your problem," Luke told him pointedly. "And you paid for it. Now it's time to move on."

"Not yet," Tom said. "The game's not over yet, is it?"

"Is that what this is to you? A game? And is Molly the grand prize?" Now Luke was getting annoyed. "She's a person, Tom. Not a thing. Not a possession. And util you learn that, you're never going to be able to grow up. And you won't be worthy of her."

They sat there in silence, watching the monitors, until Drew returned. Then Luke stood up and stretched.

"I'm going to nap for bit," he said, and started for the door.

"Hey, Luke," Tom said, stopping him.

Luke turned back and looked at him.

"I'm trying," Tom said. "Really."

"Don't tell me," Luke said. "Show her." And then he left.

Snow Miser and Heat Miser
Thursday, December 9

The snow finally stopped around mid-morning the next day. Drew had shown up with the snowmobile when it was time for Molly and Schrodinger to head home from the bookstore, and they'd gladly accepted his offer, whizzing through the falling snow again. And he'd made sure they were safely inside before heading off.

She wondered again, as she moved from dreams into a half-awake state, if he was SA. It had to be one of the Gate Techs, didn't it? There was really no one else, and lately it seemed like she couldn't turn around without tripping over one of them. And then there was Noemi's report about Tom, and the cards he'd bought. Molly felt a little guilty for hoping it wasn't him, but she couldn't help it.

If it is him, I wish he'd shown some of this creativity earlier, she thought, listening to the wind in the eaves of the house as it carried the whoops and giggles of children who didn't have to be in school playing in the three-foot snowdrifts. The house smelled of evergreens and candy canes, thanks to the Christmas tree that had been delivered Tuesday evening. Molly found she was considering spending the entire day in bed.

We could. There's nothing we need to do except make cookies, right?

Schrodinger said sleepily.

"There's dough in the freezer," Molly said, snuggling back up next to him under her flannel sheets. "We don't technically have to get up until tomorrow, if we don't want to."

Didn't you say something about going to the movies today though?

Molly frowned, trying to think. "Did I? I don't remember." She had a vague recollection of discussing the prospect with Aunt Margie yesterday, as both theaters in Carter's Cove were playing various Christmas movies all month. Maybe that had been it.

You said a Christmas movie... Schrodinger's mental voice trailed off and after a few moments, she heard him snore. She almost followed him back into sleep, but her stomach rumbled, reminding her that she needed to at least eat first.

After a very late breakfast of grilled cheese made on her homemade brioche, going back to bed just didn't seem to be the right thing to do. She let the CrossCat sleep and sat by herself in the living room, next to the decorated Christmas tree. The room lights were off and she drew the curtains on the windows, so only the flickering white lights on the tree pierced the gloom, looking like tiny stars. She'd gone simple in her decorating this year – just the white lights, and the myriad of ornaments she'd inherited over the years. There was only one new ornament – a lynx, sitting in a snowbank, his tufted ears perked, and a ribbon with the words "Schrodinger's First Christmas" at his feet. Schrodinger had been thrilled when she'd brought it out. Martha Stewart's tree it wasn't, but it was full of the things Molly loved, and that was all that mattered.

She sat and dreamed the remainder of the morning away, a mug of Christmas tea slowly cooling beside her, enjoying the stillness.

Around 1 pm, Schrodinger stuck his head into the living room. *Why didn't you nap in the bedroom with me?* He asked, waking her from her pleasant half-drowse.

"Because I wanted to see the Christmas lights, and we don't have any in the bedroom," she replied.

We could put some in there. He clambered up on to the couch, and she moved her legs to give him some room. *They could go over the headboard. It would be pretty.*

"We could." Molly considered it as she picked up her tea and sipped. It was cold, and she frowned at the mug. After a minute, it steamed again. "We still have two strands of colored lights in the Christmas box that we haven't put up yet."

Sounds like we have a plan, then.

She sat for a bit longer, looking at the lights and stroking his soft fur, then got up and stretched. "I should check the mail."

Schrodinger blinked at her wisely. *For a red envelope?*

"And the bills, among other things," Molly said, going into the kitchen and putting her boots on. She looked at her coat, then decided to go out in just her sweater. It wasn't that long a walk, after all.

Her mailbox was almost empty, except for a Christmas card from her cousin, a flyer from LL Bean, and the ubiquitous red envelope. It stirred conflicting feelings in her – part of her was still annoyed that SA hadn't announced who he was, and that she hadn't figured it out yet. But she realized that part of her had started to look forward to the daily messages, and how they were allowing her to share some of her favorite carols with Schrodinger in his first Christmas season. "I might actually miss these things once Christmas is over," she murmured to herself as she climbed the steps back into the brownstone. "Maybe I can convince SA, whoever he is, to keep them coming? Provided I figure out his identity, of course."

Did you get one? Schrodinger had come into the kitchen while she was out, and now sat in his chair at the table. She nodded, tossed the mail on the counter, and went to make him breakfast. Once he had his plate and tea, she settled in across from him and opened the envelopes.

Her cousin Charlie had sent her a hysterical card showing Santa Claus water-skiing, with a note inside teasing her about the snow. Since he'd moved to Santa Monica, he'd never lost an opportunity to remind her about the warm weather she could have been enjoying, as they'd gone to culinary school together. Molly laughed and attached it to the string with the other cards they'd received, then opened the red envelope.

SA's CD was accompanied by a pair of movie tickets and a note that said "Come with me to the movies?"

"Apparently SA read my mind, or eavesdropped on our conversation," she said to Schrodinger, getting up to put the CD in. The first notes of the song had her wrinkling her brow in confusion, but then she realized what it was and laughed. "Want to go to the movies?"

Is this from a movie? Schrodinger asked, cocking his head as he listened.

"Yes. A very, very good movie called *The Year Without a Santa Claus.* Nathan and I used to watch it ever year when it came on the TV, snuggled up next to the Christmas tree." Molly went back and looked at the tickets she'd put next to the radio. "And we have tickets for 3 p.m., which we'll make if we leave now. Want to go?"

Sure?

"You sound hesitant, cat," Molly said, pulling her coat on. "It's not that bad to walk out now. I've heard the plows go by."

It's not that, Schrodinger said. *SA sent you two tickets, right?*

"Yes." Molly waved the tickets at him. "So?"

Then it sounds like I'm not invited. Schrodinger put his head down on his front paws and sighed heavily. *It's a date just for you and SA.*

Molly went and knelt in front of him, cupping his furry face in her hands. "Except that the tickets are for the old Marshall Theatre," she told him, and his ears perked up. "And so you don't need a ticket to go see the movies there, remember? Patrick lets in you free, because he adores you. So come on, silly!"

The walk in the brisk air brought a glow to Molly's cheeks, and her heart beat a little faster as she caught sight of the Marshall Theatre, the older of the two movie theaters in Carter's Cove. It had once been a playhouse, and the screen was still on the stage. It didn't have the flashy technology of the newer cinema on the outskirts of town, but

Molly loved its old elegance, and the fact that the owners played both old and new movies. Where else could you still see Bogey and Bacall on the big screen?

There was a line in front of the ticket window, full of Cove residents queued up to see the movie. Molly saw Father Christopher, surrounded by several young children who were probably part of his Sunday school class, and her own aunt and uncle, who waved merrily at her. But who was SA? How would she know who it was?

So what do we do? Schrodinger asked, looking around.

"Join the line, I guess. SA will have to find us if he wants his seat," Molly said, slipping in at the end of the queue. She pulled the tickets out of her pocket and then jumped as someone tapped her on the shoulder.

"Going to see the movie?" Luke asked, grinning at her.

"I was planning on it," she admitted, grinning back up at him. "Or rather, my secret admirer planned it for me. Wanna join us? I have two tickets."

And I get in free! Schrodinger added. *So please join us, Luke!*

"Shouldn't SA join you?" Luke teased them. "After all, he paid for the tickets."

"How do I know you aren't SA?" Molly teased back, batting her eyelashes at him. "After all, I thought you were one of my admirers!"

"Hardly secret, though," Luke said, laughing. "I admit nothing, but I'd love to join you two."

Do you like popcorn? With butter?

"Extra butter," Luke said, and offered Molly his arm. "Shall we?"

Bring a Torch, Jeanette Isabella
Friday, December 10

One of the things Molly loved about CrossWinds Books was the little alcoves and groupings of seating that her aunt had scattered throughout both floors. Armchairs in twos and threes, some with small tables, but not all of them; cozy spots where one could sit and read, or write, or talk to friends. It was homey.

She was on one of her normal rounds of the store, checking to see if anyone needed another pot of tea or a cranberry scone, when the first clear notes of song stopped her dead in her tracks. The voice soared above the quite hum of the other customers, clear and achingly beautiful, in a wordless hymn that touched something deep inside Molly. There was peace and sorrow and acceptance and love, all at once, wrapped in the notes that floated through the air.

Once the song ended, Molly continued around the corner of the bookcase and discovered (as she had suspected) Starsha and Darian seated in one of the small conversation groupings. Starsha had just sat back in her chair, sipping on a glass of water, and Molly realized that Father Christopher had been right. It would be criminal for the girl not to become a Minstrel, and share that voice with all the realms.

"Molly! Come join us!" Darian's voice, still rich and deep, never failed to wrap around her like a warm satin robe.

"Gladly, if you two are going to continue to sing," she said, dropping into the third armchair. "Starsha, that was lovely. Did you write it?"

The Mareesh girl smiled shyly. "No, it is a traditional hymn of my people," she said, turning away slightly. "I do not write yet, but I hope to learn to. I have much learning to do."

"She is a treasure," Darian agreed, his long fingers running over the keys on the small keyboard on his lap. "And once we expand her repertoire, there will be kings begging for her to perform."

Molly had no doubt. Darian himself had performed for kings and presidents during his years traveling along the Roads before he retired to the Cove. And even now, he could be lured out by the right person. Or the right price.

"I will not only perform for the rich, though," Starsha said softly. "Music is a gift that should be shared with all the world. That is why I begged my father to let me sing in Father Christopher's holiday chorus this year. A holiday that is so saturated with music was one I must experience. I hope to enjoy many more."

"There are very few holidays that I enjoy as much as Christmas, especially here in the Cove," Darian agreed. "The music you Earth folk have come up with to celebrate this time of year is truly stupendous. Even in all my travels, I haven't seen the like."

"Really?" Molly asked. "But you've seen so much! And your people…"

"Bah. We live too long," Darian said, waving one hand in the air. "Immortality has a terrible price – boredom. And it sucks the passion out of us. Your people, on the other hand, have such vitality. It makes me feel young and whole. I will never leave the Cove again for any length of time."

"And I am excited to live here," Starsha added. "My village is very small, and our music is mostly limited to religious hymns. You have music for everything – even little things. It is wonderful."

"So you will be staying, then?" Molly asked her, and Starsha nodded.

"Darian has agreed to make me his apprentice, and my father has given his permission," the girl said. "He was saddened at first, because my birth-calling was to serve the Goddess as priestess, but Darian convinced him that I could serve this way, and our priestess agreed."

"That's wonderful!" Molly said.

Starsha smiled. "I hope so. I wish to learn so much of the music of your world. It is so very different from what I know now."

"Humans love music," Darian said. "Which reminds me." He reached into the pocket of his jeans and pulled out a red envelope, which he passed to Molly.

"I don't suppose it would do any good to ask you who gave this to you, would it?" Molly asked him.

"I believe he said to call him SA," Darian said, his dark eyes twinkling merrily.

"So you spoke to him?" Molly raised one eyebrow. "He's getting bold."

"I did, in fact." The Minstrel leaned back and grinned at her. "And no, I won't tell you who it is. You'll figure it out in due time."

"Tease," Molly grumbled, but there was no heat in her voice. "I've got it narrowed down, you know."

"Good for you." Darian gave her nothing more than that saucy grin. "You'll invite me to the wedding, yes?"

"I think you're moving a bit fast, old man." Molly laughed, opening the envelope. "Just because I think I know who it is doesn't mean there are wedding bells in my future."

"Oh, I think there are. You're a good match, and I know good matches."

"And now you're a matchmaker as well as a Minstrel?" Molly teased. "Meddling old man."

"Stubborn young woman," Darian shot back. "Hey, I need something to do in my spare time."

"I thought that's why you were taking a student," Molly said, looking at the small CD and the scrap of parchment in her hand. It read, "You are my torch in the darkness, no matter what you choose."

"I have a lot of spare time," Darian said.

Starsha was looking on with confusion writ large on her beautiful face, and Molly hastened to explain the mysterious notes she'd been receiving. Then the Mareesh laughed, clapping her hands together. "Oh, I have heard of this in tales! He will tease you, taunt you with his identity and then, once you have figured it out, will have you realize that you've fallen in love with him, yes?"

"Something like that," Molly said. "I'm not sure about the whole love part yet, though."

"That's already happened," Darian said. "You just don't know it yet."

"We'll see," Molly repeated, gathering her tea pot and getting up. Her cheeks were pink. "I have to get back to work."

Darian chuckled. "You mean you have to go listen to your CD and try to figure out who is sending them to you."

"That too," Molly said. "But I need to bake as well." She turned to Starsha. "I'm so glad to have heard you sing today, and I hope we'll see more of you here."

"I hope to see you as well," Starsha said, standing up and bowing slightly to Molly. "If you don't mind, may I come with you and listen to the music you were sent?"

"Of course."

Darian ended up following them down the stairs and into the kitchen, where Molly put the CD in and the sounds of clarinets filled the room.

"Lovely," Starsha said, when the final notes died away. "Just lovely."

Darian nodded. "As I said, humans make some of the most beautiful music." He looked at Molly. "You're very lucky."

"Because I get pretty songs?"

"Because you have people who share their inner loveliness with you," he said, and Molly realized he was serious. "Every song SA is giving you plays in his soul, and he's sharing that with you. It's a precious gift, and I hope you realize that."

Molly hadn't thought of it that way before, and after the two musicians had left, she played the song again and again, listening to it and wondering whose soul sang the haunting French words.

<><>

The bookstore smelled of cranberries and sugar and butter, warm scents that wrapped around Tom as he walked in through the front door. DC smiled at him and waved him over before he'd gotten very far.

"Molly's taken off for lunch," she said. "If that's who you're looking for."

"I'm always looking for Molly, but that's okay," he said, grinning. "Thanks for the info."

"No problem." DC looked over him critically. "You look like hell, man. Are you even sleeping?"

"Sleep is for the weak," Tom told her, and winked. "Seriously, it's just recovery. I'm fine."

He climbed the stairs to the second floor and wandered into the stacks, not really looking for anything. It was more about absorbing the feeling of the bookstore. For as long as he could remember, CrossWinds Books had been a safe haven, and he'd almost thrown it away. Twice.

"Help you find anything?"

Tom turned to see Aunt Margie standing there, a book in her hand. Her dark hair, the same color as Molly's, glowed against her crimson sweater. "No," he said truthfully. "I'm just wandering."

Aunt Margie gave him the same measured look that DC had. "Need to talk about it?"

Tom considered that for a moment. "I don't know," he said finally, leaning against the bookshelf. "I just don't know, Aunt Margie."

Aunt Margie looked up at the shelf and slid the book in, then gestured to him. "Follow me."

He'd never disobey her, so Tom followed her down into one of the corners of the building, where Aunt Margie had her office, and sank into the chair she indicated. She sat in her chair behind her desk, folded her hands, and looked at him.

"I hear things, you know," she said. "I hear things about you walking off your assignment early."

"I couldn't continue," Tom said, slumping in the chair. "It wasn't what they'd told me, Aunt Margie. It was…" His voice trailed off, and he shook his head.

"What was it?" she asked him gently, when he stopped. "You can tell me."

Those words were ones Tom had been waiting nearly a month to hear someone say, and it broke a dam in him. Before he could stop himself, before he could consider what telling her would mean, the entire story had spilled out.

"But you can't tell anyone," he said finally, when he'd finished, exhausted. "No one can know. Not even Molly. Especially not Molly."

Aunt Margie hadn't moved during his recitation, but tears stood in her blue eyes. "Molly would understand," she said softly.

"I don't even understand," Tom said, laughing a little bitterly. "How could she? How could she forgive me?"

"Because she loves you," Aunt Margie said. "Sometimes, I think she loves you more than you love yourself."

"I know she does, and I don't deserve it." Tom sighed. "But thank you."

"For what?"

"For listening." Tom pulled himself out of the chair, walked around the desk, and hugged her. "You've always listened to me, and you have no idea how much I appreciate it."

"I'll always listen," Aunt Margie told him, leaning against him. "But when will you listen to yourself?"

"Eventually, it has to sink in, right?" Tom said, giving her a lopsided grin. "Hey, do you mind doing me a favor?"

Santa Claus is Comin' to Town
Saturday, December 11

*T*hat's *who's coming today to the store? SERIOUSLY?????*

Molly laughed, even though it was hard to breathe with Schrodinger standing on her chest. He'd jumped up when she'd told him what the day held. "Yes, cat, seriously. Aunt Margie made me promise not to tell you before today, because he hadn't given her an official date for this year yet. So no one knows. But once it's announced, I'm betting there will be a line out the door!"

Can I talk to him? Can I get a picture with him? The CrossCat was all but bouncing with delight. *Will he **really** let me see him?*

"Not if you cave my chest in before we get there!" Molly shoved him backwards onto the bed, where he collapsed in a furry pile of glee. "Come on. We have to look good for our special guest."

Molly hadn't been quite honest with Schrodinger. Aunt Margie had actually pulled her aside the week before with what was going on, and since then, Molly had been making her own preparations. Night before last, she'd baked up a storm in her kitchen after she and Schrodinger got back from the movies: while he'd slept off his popcorn overindulgence, she'd made dozens and dozens of lacy snowflake cookies that she'd dusted with powdered sugar. This morning, she was planning on making more scones and tea cakes before the big arrival, and another large pot of mulled cider. That had gone over so well at the carol sing that she and Aunt Margie had agreed it might have to go on the permanent menu.

But no coffee. Molly was adamant about that. If folks wanted coffee, there was a perfectly good coffee shop run by her friends Katarina and Mick down the street in Market Square. The CrossWinds Tea Shop was just that. Tea, hot chocolate, and cider only. She'd had only one complaint in the couple of years she'd been running the shop, and the complainer had been shown the door before she'd done more than blink at him. The Cove protected its own.

The brisk walk through the predawn streets, with the dark sky glittering with millions of stars stretching above her, put her in the perfect frame of mind to bake. On mornings like this, with Schrodinger trotting beside her and the scent of sea and evergreens heavy in her nostrils, Molly couldn't imagine living anywhere else.

She let them both into the kitchen and sent Schrodinger off to scout out the perfect place to set up the chair, even though she knew Aunt Margie wanted her special guest up in front of the fireplace, bracketed by the Christmas trees. The CrossCat was practically vibrating with excitement, and she hoped the exercise would burn off some of his energy. Meanwhile, she had scones and tea cakes to make.

Aunt Margie came in about twenty minutes later, laughing. "So I guess Schrodinger knows who we're expecting today."

"Yeah, I couldn't not tell him this morning." Molly pulled a tray from the oven, full of gorgeous orange scones, and slid in a pan of tea cakes studded with raisins and walnuts. "He was thinking about not coming in, and he'd've killed me if he'd missed this event."

"What was he going to do?" Aunt Margie asked, pouring herself a cup of hot water from the copper kettle on the stove, then going into the pantry to get a tea bag.

"He said something about doing some investigating to see if he could figure out who SA is," Molly told her. "He's determined to make sure it's not a joke at my expense for the holidays."

"Oh, it's not a joke," Aunt Margie said, and Molly turned to give her aunt a raised eyebrow. "I can assure you, SA is quite serious about this."

"And you know this how?"

Aunt Margie winked at her. "Because I know who SA is, of course." And then she sailed out of the kitchen, leaving Molly gaping at her.

After a few moments, Molly shook her head and laughed. "Of course she knows who SA is. Hell, I'm probably the only one in the Cove who doesn't know yet. But that's okay. I'll figure it out eventually." She turned back to the cooling scones, touching the tops with a fingertip to make sure they were cool enough to frost. "And I've already got some clues."

Then she noticed the envelope on the island; Aunt Margie must have left it when she'd come in. Molly pulled out the CD and read the note inside. "Dear Molly, what will you ask for as your Christmas present? I know what I want. I've already sent Santa my letter. Have you? SA"

She slipped the disk into the CD player and began to mix another batch of scones, singing along to the music. It made sense that Aunt Margie knew who SA was, in retrospect – it was likely how he'd come to know so much about her. *Either that, or he's been watching me. Maybe both.*

By the time 2 p.m. arrived, Schrodinger had worked himself into a froth. Aunt Margie had called Hudson down at the Cove's radio station, and he'd announced over WCOV that there was going to be an extra-special guest arriving at the bookstore that afternoon via Doc Robbins' sleigh. The store was packed, and over the hubbub of excited children and adults, Molly heard the jingle of bells. "Schrodinger – come on!" she called, going to the kitchen door and looking out. From there, she had a straight view of the front door and saw it open, saw Aunt Margie push her way through the crowd and greet…

Santa! He's really here, Molly!

Molly's knees buckled as the CrossCat jumped up on to her shoulder from his stool, and then had to grab him before he launched himself over the crowd in his excitement. "I know, I know." She laughed at his delight. "We'll get up to see him, I promise. He stays until everyone who wants a chance gets to sit on his lap."

Even you? Will you tell him what you want for Christmas? Schrodinger leaned way over and looked her full in the face. If she hadn't had a firm grip on him, the CrossCat would have fallen on his head.

"Even me." She hadn't planned on it, but couldn't disappoint him.

And so she did. They waited until the crowd of kids thinned a little, and then Molly and Schrodinger made their way up to the second floor, where Aunt Margie had set up a large mahogany chair that Molly remembered from childhood. It had been her grandfather's, and he'd sometimes played Santa for them when they were younger, sitting in that same great chair. Aunt Margie used it every year for Santa. Molly smiled at the memories it evoked.

The Santa sitting now in the chair was no old man pretending, though, as many Santas during the Christmas season in other places were. It was obvious that there was no pillow strapped to his belly, and the white beard that flowed over his dark red robe was long, luxurious, and the very end (which brushed the pale furred edges near his black boots) wiggled as he spoke to the person on his lap. Because as Molly had told Schrodinger, it wasn't just kids who lined up to talk to him: Molly saw both Drew and Tom waiting in front of them, as well as Sue and Lai a little further up. Everyone in the Cove seemed to be packed into the store.

When it was their turn, Molly let Schrodinger jump up first. Santa leaned in and listened intently to what he said, and Molly knew it had to be serious, because Schrodinger forgot himself and his dignity enough to put a paw on Santa's chest and raise himself up to look the old elf right in the eyes. She didn't listen in, although she could have – she didn't think he'd mind. But it didn't feel right to her. This was his moment, and his alone.

And then the CrossCat accepted a candy cane from Santa, jumped down, and turned to her. *Your turn!*

Molly sat herself gingerly down on Santa's lap (which was larger than she'd expected) and looked up into his bright blue eyes.

"And what would you like for Christmas, Molly?" he asked, his voice sounding like all he did was laugh.

Opening her mouth to say something cute, Molly heard herself say, "I'd like happiness, Santa. Happiness for myself and anyone else who needs it."

"That's a big request," Santa said gravely, his eyes twinkling. "But a good one. I'll see what I can do." Then he cocked his head to one side and a smile teased the edges of his mouth. "Although I don't think I'll have to do anything. I hear you have a secret admirer."

She laughed. "Schrodinger told you!"

I did not!

Santa winked at her as he handed her a candy cane. "No, he didn't have to. Santa knows everything, you know. Enjoy your Christmas, Molly, and we'll make sure there's something special under your tree." Then he leaned in and whispered, "And you'll leave some of those peppermint snowflakes, as usual, right?"

Molly's jaw dropped. Then she blinked and said, "Of course. It's tradition."

As she walked towards the stairs, Schrodinger asked her, *What did he say to you that flustered you?*

"He asked for peppermint snowflakes," Molly said.

And that flustered you?

"We've always left peppermint snowflakes for Santa on Christmas Eve," she told him.

So? He likes them!

"I guess so." Molly decided not to try and explain any further. "It just surprised me that he remembered."

You mean people don't remember your cooking? Schrodinger looked at her, aghast.

At the end of the afternoon, Santa finally got through the last of the line and stood up from the great chair. Molly and Schrodinger were back upstairs, making sure the trays of cookies and scones were re-stocked, and saw him leave. Not through the front door, as Molly was expecting. Oh no.

Instead, Santa spread his arms wide, and said, "Merry Christmas to all!" And then he winked at those in the room, laid his finger to the side of his nose, nodded once…

And vanished.

Christmas in Killarney
Sunday, December 12

"**M**ay I join you?"

Molly looked up as Father Christopher stopped by her chair. It was another snowy Sunday in the Cove, and the store was quiet after the excitement of Saturday. She had taken advantage of the fact that she, Aunt Margie, DC, and Schrodinger were pretty much the only ones in the store to claim one of the easy chairs upstairs to read in. A small teapot with her favorite Christmas tea blend, her favorite black rose china tea cup, and a plate of lemon shortbread cookies sat on the table beside her. The only sounds other than the logs crackling in the fireplace behind her was the muted radio coming from Aunt Margie's office, and even that faded out after a moment.

She smiled up at him, closed her book and put it on the table, and then indicated the other chair. "By all means, Father. You know you're always welcome. Would you like a cup of tea?"

He sat down. "Not if it means you having to get up," he said, and she grinned at him.

"Who said anything about getting up?" Molly closed her eyes and pictured the cup she wanted. The mug currently sat on the shelf in the pantry down in the kitchen, dark brown glazed clay with golden

Norse runes painted on it. Father Christopher had told her when he gave it to her that the runes said, "Drink in health, drink in peace." She held out her hand and the mug shimmered into view. She handed it to him and then filled it from the teapot. "My gifts are practical ones, remember? As long as it has to do with a kitchen, I can bring it to myself."

Father Christopher sat back in his chair, a delighted smile on his face. "I think that's one of the many reasons I love the Cove," he said. "You see God's miracles every day."

"Pulling a tea mug from my pantry is hardly a miracle, Father," Molly said, offering him a cookie.

"What else would you call it?" He accepted the cookie. "Anything that makes someone happy is a miracle to me, and to God, and right now, this makes me very happy."

She thought about that as he sipped his tea. "I like your version of God, Father," Molly said finally.

"Me too." Father Christopher winked at her.

They sat in companionable silence for a while, listening to the crackle of the fire and the shushing of snow against the windows. With the sound system turned off, it was very quiet, like the inside of a church, Molly thought. *A church of books. Now there's a church I could worship at.* She was nominally Christian, in that very practical way that many New Englanders were. She went to church for weddings and funerals, or when she was invited to baptisms, but she didn't go regularly.

"Does God like books, Father?" she asked him, sipping at her own tea.

"Why wouldn't he?" Father Christopher said, a little startled.

"I don't know." Molly shifted a little. "It just seems like a lot of churches don't seem to like books very much anymore."

Father Christopher's face stilled for a moment, then he sighed. "Those are churches, not God," he told her. "And churches are run by people, who can interpret their faith differently. My God likes books very much."

"And yet, isn't your God the same God as theirs?" Molly shook her head. "Who do you believe?"

"Yourself," Father Christopher said firmly. "God doesn't need me or any other priest to tell you what to do. He talks directly to you in your heart. Never put your faith in churches, Molly. Listen to your heart and let Him talk to you personally."

"You'll put yourself out of business talking like that, Father," Molly teased him. "No one will come to church anymore."

"Oh, I think I'll be around for a while." Father Christopher chuckled. "I've got a lot of work to do still, and even in a magical place like the Cove, there are people who need help. But it's sometimes easier here, that's for sure. God still has work for me." He put his mug down and leaned over. "People like someone to listen to them, if nothing else."

"And who have you been listening to lately, Father?" Molly refilled both their cups.

"Oh, you know I can't tell you that. Priest-confessor confidentiality." His eyes twinkled.

"I wouldn't want you to break that," she said gravely, winking at him. "But in general? What could you possibly be hearing in a town like the Cove?"

He laughed. "More than you would believe. More than I realized." His blue eyes softened and got a faraway look. "There is so much here, Molly. So many miracles, and yet so many people are so unsure." Then he shook his head and looked back at her. "I'm hearing interesting things lately, though. Young lovers, hopeful of a Christmas miracle. Old lovers, hopeful of continued happiness. Mothers and fathers, hoping that their children will find what their hearts desire."

Molly sighed. "I wish I knew what my heart's desire was. I thought it was to be here, to run the shop, but now I'm not sure."

"Woman, and man, cannot live on tea alone," Father Christopher told her. "Even you need someone to share things with."

"Someone you might know?"

He winked at her but said nothing.

"You know, sometimes I wish I didn't have to figure these things out," Molly said. "I love reading mysteries, but I'm not good at solving the case. What if I screw this one up?"

"I don't think you can." Father Christopher finished his tea, got up and fished a red envelope out of his pocket that he handed to her. "I need to get going back to the church for evening service. Thank you for the tea, Miss Molly."

"You're welcome, Father." She smiled at him and offered the plate of cookies. "One for the road?"

"I don't mind if I do." After giving her a stately bow, he headed off down the stairs.

Molly watched him wend his way down the aisle and then turned her attention to the envelope held loosely in her hand. It was heavier than normal, and when she opened it, a beautiful bronze filigreed four-leaf clover ornament slid out, along with the CD and another note.

"Dear Molly, I found this on one of my travels, and knew it had to go on your tree. Maybe someday, we'll decorate a tree together. I hope you like it. SA"

The nave was dark, lit only by the candles surrounding the altar and burning in front of the Virgin Mary's statue in her smaller chapel. Father Christopher sat in the first row of pews, running his rosary idly through his fingers as he enjoyed the solitude. The snow was still falling outside, and he'd have to deal with the walks once more before he went in for the night, but for the moment, he just allowed himself to surrender to the peace of the Lord.

One of the doors at the back of the church opened, then closed, and he heard footsteps coming down the aisle. The newcomer genuflected to the altar, then sat down next to him.

"Things seem to be going well," Father Christopher said, when

Drew didn't say anything.

"Yes." There was something in the young man's voice, a note of worry, but he didn't say anything more.

Father Christopher knew better than to ask him directly. Sometimes, the best way to let someone know you were listening was to say nothing at all. So they sat together in the dim chapel, watching the candle flames dance, until Drew finally spoke.

"Father, can I ask you a question?"

"Of course, my son. That's what I'm here for."

Drew finally turned and looked at the priest, his hazel eyes worried. "What would you do if you knew someone had a secret, a secret that could hurt another friend very badly, but that your friend didn't know you knew, and it really wasn't any of your business? What do you do?"

"I would think it would depend," Father Christopher said after a moment. "When you say it would hurt someone badly, do you mean physically? Or emotionally?"

"Tom wouldn't hurt Molly physically," Drew said. "I know that."

"But emotionally?" Father Christopher sighed inwardly. He should have known. "Why don't you tell me what is really bothering you, Drew. It won't go any further than here, I promise you."

Drew swallowed and turned back to the altar. "A phone call came in to the Station the other day," he said quietly. "A young woman, for Tom. I didn't mean to overhear, but I couldn't help but pay attention when I heard him mention Molly's name."

"And you think maybe he is involved with this other girl?" Father Christopher said.

"He told her he loved her," Drew said. "And yes, I know, it could have been some sort of family member. It could have been anything. But it just feels...wrong."

"And it's none of your business."

"Exactly." Drew sighed. "He and Molly are just getting back to being friends. I don't want to come between them. But..." His voice trailed off.

Father Christopher put a hand on Drew's shoulder. "You're a good friend, Drew. But one of the things about being a good friend is knowing when to step back. Your first thought was right. This doesn't involve you, unless one of them comes to you."

"Being right doesn't make me feel any better," Drew said.

"I know. But you can't make their choices for them." Father Christopher squeezed his shoulder. "All you can do is be there if they need you. That's what friends do."

Walking in a Winter Wonderland
Monday, December 13

"Hey, Molly, Schrodinger, wait up!"

Molly turned as Drew came running up the sidewalk towards them. She'd just locked up the store; as she watched him come up, she wondered if he'd left something inside from earlier in the day. He and Tom had surprised her by bringing in lunch from China Gardens, and they had had an impromptu picnic party in the tea shop.

Then again, she wondered if it was something else. There had been an odd, strained couple of moments between Tom and Drew that afternoon, moments that she didn't think they'd been aware she'd noticed. Luckily, Schrodinger had seemed too enthralled with his lo mein to catch it.

"Did you forget something earlier?" she asked, as he stopped beside them.

"Sort of," he gasped, bending over to catch his breath. Schrodinger, ever the opportunist, sidled up to him and rubbed his head against Drew's shins, a purr welling up in his furry throat. "Hey, Schrodinger, how's it going? You still being good?"

Oh yes! Schrodinger said proudly. *Santa promised me my gift if I can be good until after Christmas. And I have been! I haven't even touched the new toy you put in the living room!*

Drew stood up and raised one eyebrow, confused. "What new toy I put in the living room?"

"The Christmas tree," Molly said, grinning at the look on Drew's face. "The Trio came over and helped us decorate it with my ornaments. Including mice and birds, among other things."

So tempting, Schrodinger agreed mournfully. *But that would be bad.*

"Not to mention painful," Drew said, and it was Schrodinger's turn to cock his head, the CrossCat version of an eyebrow raise. "Because there is no way any of those branches would hold your weight, buddy."

CrossCats don't fall, Schrodinger informed him.

"Except when they overshoot the island in the kitchen," Molly agreed, her grin widening.

That was ONE time, Schrodinger said, his tail lashing the cold air. *I was not myself, and I thought it was agreed that we'd never mention the incident again.*

"Aunt Margie gave him a catnip toy," Molly whispered to Drew, who laughed.

"Well, that doesn't count then," he said, leaning back over to smooth the CrossCat's ruffled fur. "And it was only once."

"So, what did you forget?" Molly said, changing the subject so as not to tease Schrodinger any more. She pulled her keys from her pocket.

"To ask what you guys were doing tonight," Drew said, standing up. "It's a beautiful night for a sleigh ride, and I've got the evening off."

As if on cue, Doc Robbins' sleigh whizzed by them, full of teenagers caroling at the top of their lungs. Molly smiled after them. "It is a lovely night, isn't it? We didn't have any plans, did we, Schrodinger? What do you say?"

You promised me a sleigh ride this winter anyways. The CrossCat looked down the road at the rapidly-moving vehicle. *Will they come back for us?*

Drew reached out for Molly's hand. "Luckily for us, I know another sleigh, a quieter one, that's nearby." The look in his hazel eyes, both hopeful and slightly worried, touched her heart and she accepted his hand.

"I think a quiet sleigh ride sounds lovely."

He led them down the street and around the corner, where Molly gasped. A small white sleigh, less than half the size of Doc Robbins', stood hitched to the glossiest white mare she'd ever seen. The sleigh itself was a silvery grey, swirled with pale blue and green trim. "Drew, it's lovely! Where did you get this?"

As he tucked them into the soft wool blankets, he grinned at her delight. "I borrowed it from Darian," he admitted. "I mentioned it was for a special trip with two very special people, and he was more than happy to let me borrow the sleigh and Cascade for a few hours."

Schrodinger wiggled in delight as Drew picked up the reins and shook them. Cascade obediently started off, pulled the sleigh smoothly along the snowy streets. It was still early enough that all the Christmas lights were on, and Drew seemed to know everywhere that had the best displays.

They went past the elementary school, where the monument of the *Daughter of Stars*, Captain Carter's ship, was decked in white twinkling lights. The Station, perched up on the outskirts of the town by the cliffs, was covered with lights that looked like icicles and candy, and Molly wondered where Mal had found them. Most houses had lights in their windows and winding around porches and doorways, and Schrodinger was enthralled. For herself, it was like being a child again, snuggled in the warm blankets and seeing the lights for the first time. Molly decided then and there that she and Schrodinger would have to do this every year he was here.

The CrossCat looked back at her as he caught that thought. *As long as I'm here?* The echo held a bit of confusion. *Why wouldn't I be here?*

Because you might want to travel on, Molly thought back at him, not wanting to bring Drew into the private conversation. *Don't all CrossCats travel?*

Most do, he agreed. *But I'm not most CrossCats.*

That she couldn't disagree with.

"Molly," Drew said, breaking into her thoughts. "Are you still having your dinner party tomorrow night?"

"Yes," she said, looking over at him. "Why? Did Mal say you had to work?" A brief pang shot through her. The party wouldn't be the same without him.

"Oh, no," he assured her. "Mal knows that if we aren't allowed to go, he doesn't get any more goodies this week. It's not that."

"Then what?" Molly wondered again if it had to do with Tom.

"Did Tom say he was coming?" Drew didn't look at her as he asked the question.

"Yes, he said he would." Molly frowned. "Why?"

There was silence for a couple of moments, and even Schrodinger turned to look at the Gate tech.

"It's not..." Drew broke off, and sighed. "It's nothing. Forget I said anything. I'm just tired – it's been a long week."

Molly blinked, but let it drop after a confused look at Schrodinger. "I'll bet, considering the Snow Queen's Ball is Saturday. The Gate must be rocking."

"Yes, it is." Drew grinned at her, the odd moment gone. "Which means we can't be out too late tomorrow night."

"I'll make sure you're home on time," she teased him. "Can't make Mal too angry, or he might not let you out again!"

They laughed together, the mood lightened, and Drew turned down their street. He pulled the sleigh up in front of her brownstone.

"Thank you," Molly said, climbing out of her warm cocoon reluctantly. Schrodinger snuggled up against Drew in thanks, then jumped down beside her. "See you tomorrow night?"

"I wouldn't miss it," Drew said, then he winked at her. "Is that all the thanks I get?"

"You could come up for cookies," Molly said, grinning at him.

"Sadly, I can't – gotta get Cascade back to her owner."

"Well, then, I guess you'll have to settle for this." Molly climbed back up and leaned over to give him a chaste sisterly kiss on the cheek. "I'll see you at 8 p.m. tomorrow, then."

Drew waited until she'd opened the front door, then waved and drove the sleigh off down the street.

That was so much fun! Schrodinger said, bouncing up the stairs. *We should do it again!*

"It was," Molly agreed, and then stopped, looking at her door. There, tucked next to the bird house in the wreath, was another red envelope. Inside was the mini CD and a note which read, "Molly, I hope you enjoyed your sleigh ride. You looked lovely with the wind whipping through your hair. SA"

"How did it go?" Darian asked, stepping into the stable. Drew, who was rubbing Cascade down, turned and smiled at him.

"It was amazing," he said. "Thank you again."

Darian leaned against the door frame, watching him get the mare ready to bed down for the night. "You know you're always welcome to borrow her," the Minstrel said. "And it's not like I'm traveling at the moment. Even if I'm not here, you now know where everything is."

Drew gave the mare once last stroke with the cloth in his hand and then let himself out of her stall.

"You're troubled, though," Darian said, and Drew looked sharply at the elf. "Did you have an argument with someone?"

"Only myself," Drew said, putting the cloth away. He sighed and shook his head. "Things are complicated."

"Life usually is, I've found," Darian said. "Do you want to talk about it?"

"Not really, but thank you." Drew had thought long and hard after his conversation with Father Christopher the other night. He was still concerned about Tom, but the priest had been right. It didn't involve him. And he'd be there if Molly needed a shoulder to cry on.

"You're a good friend, Drew," Darian said quietly. "Just don't forget to take care of yourself."

"Myself?" Drew asked. "I'm fine."

The Minstrel smiled at him. "Good. I hope it remains that way." He pushed himself off the door frame and stretched. "I think it's time for a bit of music now. Join me, if you would like." And without waiting for an answer, Darian turned and left.

Santa Baby
Tuesday, December 14

The dinner party, Molly decided, was a complete success.

She looked around her small living room in satisfaction. They'd moved her long coffee table to the center of the room, shoved the couch against the wall, and Lai had brought over nearly a dozen large pillows to use as seats. Only the lights on the Christmas tree and the white votive candles guttering down the length of the table lit the room, but that didn't dim the conversation glittering in the air.

Lai, Sue, Noemi, Tom, Drew, Luke, and Luke's younger brother Zach all lounged around the table with her, all holding drinks. Tom had taken his customary position within the group as bartender back, showing up with a long board that they'd placed on the couch cushions and a selection of top-shelf liquors and mixers. Schrodinger was cuddled up in Sue's lap, already almost asleep but refusing to give in to his tiredness for fear that he might miss something. Sue stroked his head with one hand as she chatted with Zach about the University of Maine at Orono, where he was a junior majoring in museum sciences. Tom, Noemi, and Luke were discussing the Red Sox's newest acquisition, and Lai and Drew were debating the pros and cons of something esoteric that she only caught a few hints about. From the look in Lai's eyes, it was probably art-related, but Molly wasn't sure and didn't really care. For herself, she was just listening to everything and enjoying the feelings of camaraderie that permeated the apartment.

The guys had been in charge of bringing drinks and appetizers, and besides the bar, they had shown up with bruschetta and a shrimp ring with a very spicy cocktail sauce that was part of Luke's family recipes. The Trio had provided dessert, which was still sitting in the refrigerator, and Molly had contributed dinner: a roast leg of lamb, redolent with rosemary, mint, and raspberries; a bowl of fluffy, buttery mashed potatoes; and minted carrots to round out the meal.

This is the best way to spend a winter's evening, she thought, swirling the remains of her rum and coke in her glass. *Good food, good friends, and good conversation.*

Agreed, came Schrodinger's contented thought.

"So, Molly, did you get a carol from SA today?" Lai asked suddenly, turning around.

"I did!" Molly said, putting her glass down. "Hang on and I'll get it." She went into the kitchen, collected the small CD that had shown up on her wreath earlier that day, and brought it back into the living room. "So today, SA hit a home run out of the park. He actually not only found my favorite carol of all time, but my favorite version of it as well."

"Oh?" Tom asked, and the others all looked at her. "What did he send you?"

Molly didn't answer him. Instead, she put the mini CD into the stereo system by the TV. As the music filled the room, her feet began to move in time to the beat, even though Molly never really danced, or sang, or anything like that anymore. She hadn't been lying when she'd said this was her absolute favorite Christmas carol, and she could never resist singing along with Eartha Kitt, although she couldn't match her sultry tones.

Lai and Noemi jumped up to join her, and the three of them

pirouetted and posed as the strains of "Santa Baby" echoed through the air. When the carol ended, the others erupted into applause.

"Damn, I'm bringing booze over more often, if that's the reward," Tom said, as Molly collapsed beside him, still laughing.

Surprisingly, this time, the words didn't sound possessive, and Molly just laughed harder at him. "What makes you think you're going to get the chance?" she teased. "I might not invite you to the next dinner party I throw!"

He fell backwards, clutching at his chest in mock-agony. "Oh, the pain of rejection!" he cried, but Molly didn't hear anything other than laughter in his voice. No anger, which made her happy. She didn't want to argue with Tom any more.

Everyone laughed again, and when they'd calmed down a bit, Luke said, 'You know, though, Molly, I don't think I've ever seen you do that."

"That's because she's got stage fright, so she won't go out with us to karaoke," Sue told him. "I think it's the booze tonight."

"The booze, and the song," Molly admitted. "It really is my favorite."

She's been singing it all afternoon, Schrodinger agreed.

"It's not just that," Luke insisted. "You've never worn anything like this either." He looked her up and down and added, "It suits you. I like it."

"Agreed," Drew and Tom said, and Zach nodded.

Molly blushed. The red sequined tank top was very much not her normal style, but she'd fallen in love with it on an infrequent shopping trip to Freeport, and this was the first chance she'd had to wear it. Paired with skinny blue jeans, Molly felt like a model. Even in bare feet. "Thanks," she said. "I figured since we were having an adult-type dinner party, I should dress up."

"Speaking of dinner, this was incredible," Drew said, and everyone nodded. "But I have to ask – what's for dessert?"

Molly laughed. "The girls brought tiramisu," she said. "Help me clear the table, Tom, and we can bring it out."

Everyone ended up helping bring dishes and the leftovers (what little there were) out to the kitchen, where Molly pulled the tiramisu from the refrigerator and ladled it into dessert cups, which Tom handed around. The simple action reminded her of other parties they'd held together, back when this had been their apartment, but this time, the thought didn't send a shot of anger through her. Maybe it was the rum.

Or maybe we're both finally growing up, she thought, watching Tom tease Sue, who had finally levered Schrodinger off her lap and joined them. *Maybe it's time we both moved on.*

Her gaze wandered over to Drew, who was leaning back against the wall with his dessert. He looked at her at the same time, and gave her a slow wink, then turned back to Noemi and continued his conversation. Next to him, on the kitchen table, was the red envelope the CD had come in earlier.

SA's words came back to her. "Be happy, Molly. Enjoy the day, and don't be afraid to be you. You don't do that often enough."

Don't be afraid to be you. Molly scooped out the last of her tiramisu and grinned. *It's good advice, and I think I'm going to follow it.*

<><>

Out of the corner of his eye, Luke watched Molly grin. It was a brief, private smile; she was obviously amused by her own thoughts, and didn't think anyone else would see. And really, everyone else seemed to be concentrating on their dessert or the conversations that swirled around him, so it had been a fairly safe bet.

Then again, he hadn't really been able to stop watching her all night. It hadn't just been the outfit, although that had been flashy enough. She'd just seemed happier than she'd been in a long time, sparkling in the dim light of the candles and the Christmas tree, outshining everyone else there.

Which meant, of course, that now Luke was pondering just how unhappy she'd been, and why he hadn't really seen it before. Molly's words about how they'd all treated her as a sister were truer than he'd like to believe, although Luke knew why he'd kept his distance.

Tom laughed at something Sue said, which pulled Luke's attention from Molly to them. Tom had never been one to stop going for what he wanted, something Luke had envied at one point. For a while, he'd thought (along with most of the Cove) that Tom and Molly were meant for one another.

Once the break-up had happened, Luke had thought maybe he'd have a chance to ask Molly out. But it never seemed to be the right time.

Or you never had the guts, he thought to himself, his gaze going back to where Molly was pulling out a kettle and setting it on the stove. She was laughing, teasing Zach about how he was going to eat her out of house and home if he kept coming over. Just like a big sister should.

You should ask her out again, Schrodinger said, surprising him. Luke looked down to see the CrossCat lounging against his leg, a tiramisu glass licked clean in front of him. *She had a lot of fun.*

I did too, Luke thought. *With both of you.*

So why don't you ask her again?

I don't know, Luke admitted. *Maybe because I'm afraid she'll say no?*

Why would she? Schrodinger looked up at him. *You're a good friend, and she likes spending time with you.*

A good friend. Luke wondered if he'd ever be anything else. Or if he wanted to be.

You're a Mean One, Mr. Grinch
Wednesday, December 15

Schrodinger curled up in his bed next to the fireplace on the upper level of CrossWinds Books and dozed, idly contemplating the universe. Specifically, the slice of universe that he could see without moving his head from his front paws, which happened to include Drew and Tom as they sat in a pair of easy chairs, talking in low tones, and Doc Robbins, who was also snoozing, although he had a magazine open on his lap.

It didn't matter that the two young men were across the room from him, and that the fire was crackling merrily behind him – if he'd wanted to, he could have listened into their conversation. CrossCats had a number of talents, and the ability to hear across the Roads was one vital to their survival. But he'd been taught to be polite long before he'd come to the Cove, and there was nothing that really concerned him anyways.

So he basked in the warmth and daydreamed, content to listen to the soft Celtic harp Christmas music Aunt Margie had playing on the sound system, ignoring the bits and pieces of conversation that swirled around him. Or at least, until the word "Molly" pierced his semi-sleep. Especially as it was said in a very urgent whisper.

Without moving his head to give away that he'd heard anything, Schrodinger swiveled his ears slowly, seeking out the voice he'd heard. His eyes, only open a slit, saw Drew and Tom, still talking, and Aunt Margie and Father Christopher, standing by the stacks and also deeply involved in a conversation. Who had it been?

Hard to tell, since it had been a whisper and he heard both Aunt Margie and Drew say her name within moments of one another. Since he didn't worry about Aunt Margie much, Schrodinger decided to concentrate his attention on the two Gate techs.

"Look, I know it's none of my business," Drew was saying. "I barely know you."

"Which is true," Tom said.

"But I do know Molly," Drew continued, and Schrodinger's mental eyebrows rose. "And I know that she deserves to know the truth after this. Especially if she makes the choice you want her to." He paused, then added, "Luke agrees with me on this."

Tom sighed. "It's more complicated than that, Drew. And it really is none of your business. Or Luke's."

"It is when I'm having to cover for you with Mal, because you are nowhere to be found," Drew replied. "And it's Luke's when he's taking messages for you at all hours of the night. What is going on?" When Tom didn't answer right away, Drew added, "If nothing else, how can you expect Molly to choose you if you're seeing someone else on the side?"

"I'm not seeing anyone!" Tom hissed. "I never cheated on Molly!"

"That's not what I've heard," Drew said, his hazel eyes glittering. "And if you aren't, who is this girl who keeps calling you?"

Tom hesitated, and before he could answer, Schrodinger heard Aunt Margie say, "Besides, she's finally getting into the secret admirer game, and I haven't seen her so happy since Tom left. She's acting like Molly again. I hear the dinner party was a great success."

"Which is a blessing," Father Christopher agreed. The two were far enough away from Drew and Tom that the boys' whispered conversation probably couldn't be heard, but Schrodinger watched as the priest eyed the two Gate techs. "I was worried that she'd shut herself away from Tom. Especially after the blow up they had last week."

"That was his fault," Aunt Margie said tartly, but then her face softened as she too glanced at the boys. "He's always thought that she'd be there for him, no matter what. And he's right. But it's as a friend, not anything more, no matter what he wants."

"I just hope he realizes that."

"He's getting there," Aunt Margie said. "There are other things going on with Tom, and while this secret admirer game is keeping the rest of the town occupied with Molly, it's giving him some time to work some things out. We had a long talk the other day."

"I'm glad he's talking to someone." Father Christopher looked happier. "I was worried about him."

"A lot of us were." Aunt Margie shook her head.

Schrodinger pondered that as he sat there listening. Tom had picked up his book and was determinedly reading it, while Drew was texting someone, his brow furrowed. So the CrossCat returned his attention to Aunt Margie and Father Christopher.

"She's still planning on coming to the Snow Queen's Ball on Saturday, right?" Father Christopher said.

"Yes. We're closing the store early, of course, and she even bought a dress yesterday. She's going to look like a princess."

"And SA will be there," Father Christopher said, leaning back and putting his hands on his belly. "Do you think she's guessed who it is yet?"

"She says she hasn't, although I think she's got suspicions." Aunt Margie chuckled. "But then again, if she hasn't at least got some suspicions by now, then she's blind. And that's one thing Molly isn't, usually."

"Unless she wants to be, no. What about SA – does he know what he needs to do that night?" Father Christopher asked.

Aunt Margie laughed. It was a bright sound, very much like Molly's – one of Schrodinger's favorite sounds, truth be told.

"That boy has known what he was going to do since the day he came up with this scheme," she said. "I have no doubt that anything he sets his mind to, he'll get."

"She could still say no," Father Christopher reminded her.

"She could, but she'd be a moron to." Then Aunt Margie sighed. "No, actually, then she'd be the Molly we all know and love. Always too willing to put others and their feelings ahead of herself to see how it's negatively affecting her life. She'd want to spare any hard feelings."

That, at least, Schrodinger could agree with. He loved Molly, but she didn't want to seem to want to take care of herself very much. That's why he'd asked Santa for someone for her. It sounded like Aunt Margie and Father Christopher may have done the same thing, and SA was the result.

He was still staring at Drew and Tom as he thought, and although his eyes saw what happened next, his brain didn't quite catch it. Or didn't realize it. He wasn't sure which. Drew and Tom looked at each other, apparently coming to some sort of agreement, and shook hands. A flash of red flickered in between them. It could have been a small envelope that was passed between them, but Schrodinger couldn't be sure. What he was sure of was that both Drew and Tom stood up, adjusted their coats, and walked out. Not together – Tom headed into the stacks, the book still in his hand, while Drew went towards the stairs.

So it IS one of them, Schrodinger thought. *Unless someone gave them that envelope. After all, Father Christopher has gotten some.* He shifted in his bed, pondering that. *No, I think it's one of them.* Then his mind gave him a picture of Luke, pulling up on the snowmobile and showing up at the movie theater, and he sighed. *I wish I could figure it out. I could help...*

Then his head came up. *I COULD help!*

Schrodinger jumped up and trotted over to where Father Christopher was now sitting alone, Aunt Margie having gone to attend to something or other. The chair she'd been sitting in was still warm, and Schrodinger leaped gracefully up into it.

"Hello, Schrodinger," the priest said, closing the book he'd been reading. It was large, with an elaborate picture on the front of some sort of medieval tapestry, Schrodinger thought, but the book didn't interest him as much as it might have otherwise. "How is your day going?"

Good, Father, Schrodinger said politely, sitting up straight and wrapping his tail around his paws. *I need to talk to you.*

"Oh? About what?" Father Christopher looked a little surprised at the seriousness in the CrossCat's mental voice.

Schrodinger leaned forward until his nose almost touched the priest's. *I want to help.*

Father Christopher blinked. "Help with what?"

I want to help SA win Molly, Schrodinger said, and Father Christopher's eyes went guarded. *I know you know who he is, and that you think he'd be good for her. I trust you, so he must be. And so I want to help.*

"You do, do you." Father Christopher regarded him thoughtfully for a few moments, chewing on his bottom lip. "But tell me, Schrodinger, can you keep a secret from her? Because that's what it's going to take until she figures it out on her own."

I can, he said, nodding. *CrossCats are good at secrets.*

"And if she asks you who it is?" Father Christopher pressed. "Could you tell her that you didn't know, even if you did?"

No, Schrodinger admitted. *But I won't have to. I don't want to know who he is. I just want to help deliver things, and those, I can get through you or Aunt Margie.* He cocked his head as a thought occurred to him. *Unless you're SA, of course. But don't you think Molly's a little young for you?*

Father Christopher laughed at that. "The Holy Father might have issues if I started chasing young ladies, so I can promise you, it's not me," he said. "But I'll let him know you want to help. That's all I can do. It's up to him."

Schrodinger nodded. *Good. Thank you.*

Baby, It's Cold Outside
Thursday, December 16

"You do realize I haven't been skating in years, right?"

Drew laughed as they laced up their stakes. "That's okay, I haven't either," he assured her. "But I saw the ad in the *Covenant*, and I thought it would be fun. Especially since I've never skated on anything but an indoor rink."

They were seated on a log, lacing up rented skates. Carter's Cove had plenty of ice around, being right on the ocean, but not much of it was good for skating, which is why anyone who wanted to skate went to one of the rivers leading into the Cove. There were three total, but it was the gentle Elizabeth River, named for Captain Carter's favorite granddaughter, that Drew had brought Molly and Schrodinger to. In a sheltered cove, India Sarabian and her husband had brushed the snow from the ice and built a roaring bonfire on the beach. Logs dragged out from their farm (which perched on a cliff above the river) provided benches, and India herself had built a small stand, complete with generator, to provide hot and cold beverages and food for sale. There was no charge to just come and skate, and India had skates for rent as well. Stars glittered overhead and instead of spotlights, there were masses and masses of Christmas lights strung through the trees that lined the cove. The inlet itself was nearly circular, and the ice was as smooth as glass.

Molly looked over at Schrodinger, who was watching them and the skaters with interest. "I think you should stay here on the beach," she said. "I don't want you getting cut or run over out there."

I think I shall, he agreed. *Besides, it's warm here next to the bonfire, and there are enough people here to keep me company.*

That there were. Molly looked around the cove: there were people everywhere, mostly younger folks, although her aunt and uncle were already on the ice, skating together like they must have forty years ago when they were dating. She smiled as she watched them. It was apparent to everyone how much they still loved each other.

Schrodinger nudged her hand with his head, and when she looked down, he purred encouragingly. *You'll find someone like that. I know you will.*

"You do, huh?" She scratched his head. "I wish I shared your convictions."

"Coming?" Drew asked her, and she looked up to see him standing in front of her, holding out his hand. He helped her to her feet, and then they walked slowly through the snow to the edge of the river.

Molly took a deep breath and stepped out on to the glassy ice. Her skates slipped a bit, but Drew still had her hand and helped her steady herself.

"Thanks," she said, leaning on him a little as her legs tried to remember how to stand on skates. "Like I said, it's been a few years."

"We'll take it slow," he promised, drawing her farther out onto the ice. Despite what he'd said, Drew didn't seem to have any rust on his skills at all, skating backwards as he led her out onto the ice with nary a wobble of his blades. "It's just like riding a bike," he continued, and Molly found he was right. "You just have to remember how to move."

After a few uncertain moments, she felt a little more steady and Drew moved beside her, tucking her hand under his arm. They skated around the cove for a time in silence, enjoying the carols playing over the sound system. Molly caught glimpses of Schrodinger from time to time; he was curled up on a cushion that one of India's young sons had brought out for him, accepting caresses from any and all that offered them. He had no shortage of folks willing to sit with him.

"Penny for your thoughts?" Drew said after their second circuit.

"None, really," Molly admitted "It's a beautiful night, and I'm just enjoying it." She smiled up at him. "Thank you."

"No, thank you," he said. "I'm glad you came out."

"I've gone out more this month than I have in the past six," she said. "You guys have been pretty persuasive."

"Good. God knows we've been trying." Drew grinned at her. "Have you figured out who your secret admirer is yet?"

"I have my suspicions," she said. "Luke all but admitted it was one of you three, which I think is adorable. Weird, but adorable."

Drew shook his head in mock dismay. "Luke never could keep a secret from a pretty girl."

Molly laughed. "You guys are too much. I don't know why you all felt the need to go through this, though, whichever one of you it is. It's fun, but isn't it a lot of work?"

"You're worth it," Drew said instantly. "And besides…" He hesitated and Molly wondered why. "Besides, after last summer…"

"Tom and I had a lot of issues," Molly said, cutting him off. "Not the least of which was that we didn't talk to one another about anything."

"Tom doesn't like to talk much," Drew agreed. "He's much more of an action guy."

"Yes, he is." Molly didn't say anything more, and another silence fell between them. But it wasn't an uncomfortable one, like she'd thought it might be. Just a quiet one. She realized that she liked being with Drew, even when they didn't talk.

"Your aunt said you bought a dress for the Snow Queen's Ball," Drew said finally, after a few minutes.

Molly grimaced. "You'd think I'd never bought a dress before, the way she's been carrying on about it. It's just a dress, I promise."

"Considering I've heard how formal the Snow Queen's Ball is, I doubt it's just a dress," Drew said. "Any clues on the color, or do I have to pump your aunt for more information?"

"She hasn't seen it," Molly said. "No one has, except Schrodinger, and he's been sworn to secrecy. I went to Portland for it." She looked up at him again, cocking one eyebrow. "Why do you want to know the color?"

"So I can get you a corsage to match it, silly," he said, and she actually stopped in her tracks, staring at him. "What?"

"Buy me a corsage? Seriously?"

"Yes, seriously." Drew tugged her hand, pulling her into motion again. "Why is that so weird?"

"Because the only folks who buy corsages for people are ones who are together," Molly said. "Like married couples."

"Not true. I used to buy my mother a corsage for Christmas and Easter every year." Drew sighed. "Right up until the year she died. I'd save all my allowance for it."

"I'm sorry." Drew didn't talk much about her family, and Molly had to bite her lip not to ask any more questions. "White," she told him.

"What?" he said, blinking a little at the non sequitor.

"My dress is white," she said softly. "With pale blue accents."

Drew looked down at her, with her long dark hair blowing back in the wind, and said, "Of course it is. You're going to outshine the Snow Queen herself."

"Not hardly," Molly scoffed. "No one outshines her. Trust me, you'll see."

"I'm looking forward to it."

They took a short break to check on Schrodinger and warm up a bit, then Drew tugged her back out onto the ice. Molly was certain her legs would be sore the next day, but it was worth it to be out on the ice, the cold bringing roses to her cheeks.

India's voice came over the PA system. "Last skate, folks. I need to get my kids to bed, and this is too loud for them to sleep, so we've got one more song. This one is dedicated to Molly, according to the envelope I have here for her. Molly, when you return your skates, I'll give it to you."

Molly giggled. "I wondered where my envelope was." She cocked her head at Drew. "And just how did SA know we were going to be here tonight?"

"SA seems to have a good information network," he said slyly, winking at her. "Did you have any other plans for tonight? It's not that late."

"I should go home," she admitted, as the first notes of the song "Baby, It's Cold Outside" floated across the ice. "I still need to frost brownies for tomorrow."

"Do you have to?" he asked, and she nodded.

"But you could come help me," she said, looking up at him. "I'd like help."

"I'd be happy to."

They picked up her envelope, which contained not only the CD but a pretty silver skate ornament, and collected Schrodinger, who was thrilled that Drew was coming back with them. *All in all,* Molly thought, snuggling against the seat in his truck, *it's been one heck of a night.*

She glanced over at Drew, who was making sure Schrodinger was comfortable before he pulled out. *And I have a feeling it's just getting started.*

Blame It on the Mistletoe
Friday, December 17

"So, spill it. What time did he leave?"

Molly grinned at Sue, who was perched on one of the stools at the island. "Are you going to be disappointed if I tell you he left around midnight, after helping me frost brownies?"

"Is that what you're calling it now?" Sue quirked her fingers into air quotes. "Frosting brownies?"

"Hahaha." Molly threw a raspberry from the bowl in front of her at her best friend, who popped the morsel into her mouth. "No, really. We frosted brownies and talked. You can ask Schrodinger – he was there."

"Did he at least try to kiss you?" Sue asked. "Because if he didn't, I'll be disappointed in both of you." She cocked her head at Molly. "So, did he?"

"Well…" Molly said, pretending to concentrate on the frosting she was mixing up. Then she laughed, unable to string her friend along anymore. "Feel free to be disappointed in both of us, because he didn't, and neither did I. Not a real kiss, anyways. I got a very nice kiss on the forehead before he left, though."

"What? The forehead?" Sue grabbed another berry and crunched viciously into it. "That bastard."

"Because he didn't kiss me?" Molly's laughter rang out again over the carols playing on the kitchen's CD player. "Really, Sue, you should be happy he's a gentleman."

Sue muttered something that Molly didn't catch, then sighed. "I suppose you're right, but dammit, I heard how cozy the two of you were at India's last night. You can't really get more romantic than skating together, and according to the rumor mill, Drew never left your side. Why didn't he capitalize on that?"

"Probably because he's smart enough to know that if he pushes too fast, I'll shove him off the boat," Molly said. "You know that. I hate to be pushed into anything. Drew knows I have my own pace."

"Do you think SA is him?" Sue asked.

"I think it's a pretty good possibility," Molly admitted.

"So what if he's not?" Sue said. "Would you choose him, instead of SA?"

The question hung in the air between them. Molly didn't answer immediately, because she honestly wasn't certain of what she would do if Drew wasn't SA. What if it was Luke? Or Tom? Or someone else she hadn't even considered? The problem was, every time she started to think like that, her stomach gave an odd little flip.

"I don't know," she said finally. "Maybe I'm not in love with any of them. Maybe I'm just in love with the idea of a secret admirer. Gods, that would suck, wouldn't it? How horrible that makes me sound."

And then she heard an apologetic cough, and both she and Sue looked up to see Luke standing in the doorway. She looked into his green eyes and her stomach gave that little flip again, although she wasn't sure if it was pleasure at seeing him or embarrassment that he'd obviously overheard her. "Hey," she said, blushing a bit.

Luke chuckled at her expression. "Am I welcome here, or intruding?"

"Not intruding." Molly surrendered to her embarrassment and waved him in. "Come on over before I stick my foot further into my mouth."

"You didn't. You were being honest," Luke said, coming in and snagging one of the other stools. He winked at both of them. "Besides, you didn't say you weren't interested in having a relationship. Just that you weren't sure. That still gives me hope."

"Are you admitting to something?" Sue pounced on his words.

"Sure. Thinking Molly's a gorgeous, sexy lady." Luke grinned at her expression. "That's no secret." When Sue pouted at him, he laughed. "You aren't getting me to admit to anything else yet, Sue. This little game isn't done yet, and if I blow the story, well, that won't be fun for anyone."

"Is that what you consider this? Fun?" Sue said.

"Isn't it?" Luke said. He turned to Molly. "Aren't you having fun?"

"Are you here to visit or to tease?" Molly countered, bringing a tray of cooled cupcakes over to the island. She then filled the icing bag and began to carefully pipe little red stars on top of the first cupcake.

"A little of both," Luke admitted. "I wanted to stop in and see you, and I brought you a present. But I'll never pass up the chance to tease you – you should know that." He reached down into the bag at the feet and brought out a smallish box. It was about the size of a box one might give a mug or a tea cup in, and Molly's eyes widened. Her fondness for mugs and cups was well-known. His next words, however, confused her. "I know you have a wreath and a tree, but I really think you need one of these as well. To round out your Christmas decorations."

Molly and Sue exchanged dubious glances, but Molly put down her icing bag and picked up the box. It was lighter than she'd expected. Curiouser and curiouser. She opened the flap and lifted out a ball of evergreens and holly berries, tied with a bright red ribbon.

"A kissing ball!" Sue said, clapping her hands. "Oh, Molly, you have to hang it up!"

"Here?" Molly shot Sue an amused look. "Aunt Margie might not appreciate the line of folks who want to kiss in the kitchen underneath it. Never mind what the health department would say."

"Considering the Health Inspector knows you personally and

knows how clean you keep this kitchen, I doubt it would be a problem," Sue said. "Besides, it's not like kissing is a dirty habit."

"No, kissing is definitely not a dirty habit." Luke took the kissing ball from Molly's fingers, got up from the stool, walked around the island to stand next to her and held it over her head. "Is it?"

Molly forgot about the cupcakes waiting to be frosted, forgot about Sue sitting on the other side of the island, forgot about everything except the taste of Luke's mouth on hers as he leaned down and kissed her. This was not the boy she'd grown up around and played with; this was a man, one that had matured while she wasn't looking. Aunt Margie could have marched Carter High's jazz quartet through the kitchen and she wouldn't have noticed. Time slowed and then stopped entirely as Luke reminded her exactly what a gentle, thorough kiss could do to her.

Then he stepped back, handed her the kissing ball and, tipping his newsboy cap to both of them, grabbed his bag and left. He nodded at Aunt Margie as he passed her in the doorway.

"Molly?" Aunt Margie started to say something else, and then looked at her niece closely. "Are you okay?"

Her knees were buckling. Nodding dumbly, Molly sank down onto the stool she'd pushed aside earlier, looking at the kissing ball in her hands.

Sue laughed. "She's just been well and truly kissed, Aunt Margie. Give her a few minutes to recover."

"Ah, he's a good kisser, then?" Aunt Margie nodded in satisfaction. "Good. That's always important." She laid down the red envelope she'd brought in and nodded again. "Very important."

Molly wet her lips and finally found her voice. "I didn't know he could do that."

"That's because you still see him as the boy you went fishing with," Aunt Margie told her. "Boys grow up."

"Yes they do." Molly blinked and finally broke the spell. She laid the kissing ball back in its box and closed the lid. "I think that might go home with me, though. I'm not sure I'll be able to get my job done otherwise."

Both Aunt Margie and Sue laughed again. "Too distracting?" Sue teased.

"I'll tell you what, you can take it and go kiss him," Molly said, blushing again. "And then you can tell me if it's distracting."

"Oh no, I'll not disrupt SA's plans," Sue said, and Molly noticed a slight reddening of her friend's cheeks. "But you can only choose one of them. Maybe I'll get a chance to try later…"

"Why, Sue Elder, are you sweet on Luke?" Molly teased, and watched her friend flush darker. "You are! Why haven't you said anything?"

"Because as is patently obvious, he isn't interested in me," Sue pointed out.

"You don't know that." Molly stowed the kissing ball in her own bag, and then went back to the neglected cupcakes. "I wouldn't take anything I think I know for granted anymore."

"True," Sue said, popping another raspberry in her mouth. "I guess we'll just have to see."

"I guess we will," Molly agreed.

The Christmas Waltz
Saturday, December 18

Molly took one last deep breath and looked down at her date. "Ready, Schrodinger?"

I was born ready. The CrossCat rubbed a paw across his black bow tie and then stretched. *Let's go astonish them with our elegance.*

Elegant was not how Molly was feeling, sitting in her sister-in-law's car and staring out at the path to the ballroom. Terrified was more like it. She reached up to touch her hair, hoping the intricate braiding hadn't already started to fall, and the subtle scent of starflowers wafted over her. Once again, she looked at the corsage Drew had sent to her, and wondered just how far she was willing to go on this journey.

He hadn't delivered it himself; Father Christopher had, explaining that the tech had been so busy at the Station that he hadn't been able to get away. "Besides," the priest had said, smiling, "I had another present for you as well, left at the Church."

That had been another red envelope, of course, containing a lovely version of "The Christmas Waltz" and the simple words, "I hope you'll dance with me tonight."

Molly wondered, for the nth time, if she was right in thinking who her secret admirer was. He wouldn't admit it, not even tonight –

not until Christmas, she knew, in keeping with the Advent calendar theme he'd chosen. But dammit, what if it wasn't who she thought…

"Enough," she said out loud, tucking the keys into her purse and smoothing the front of her dress. "It's just my friends out there, after all."

Well, no, technically, it's the entire town, plus whoever else the Snow Queen decided to invite, Schrodinger said helpfully, jumping out of the car. *But most of them like you. At least, the ones who know you do.*

"You aren't helping, Cat," she said, getting out of the car and picking up the edges of her skirts. She had gone all out on her dress, and moving in it over the packed snow was interesting, to say the least. At least she'd gotten sensible flats to wear with it. Not that anyone would see her shoes, not with the floor-length skirts. Skirts that shimmered with the palest blue and silver beads she'd ever seen, which had drawn Molly to the dress in the first place. It was so far outside what she normally wore that she felt like a different person standing in the snow outside the glade where the Snow Queen held her annual ball.

Molly didn't know the Snow Queen's real name – she had only ever seen her at the ball, although Aunt Margie sometimes sent books to the Winter Palace, along one of the more stable Roads. The Snow Queen did not encourage guests, normally – she was a quiet neighbor, and rarely ventured out of her own domain. But every year, on the Saturday night before Christmas, the Snow Queen set up a magical circle in a large glade in the forest outside of the Cove proper, and threw a ball. The town's oldest residents said it was to thank the Cove for keeping the entrance to her kingdom safe during the Second World War, but Renae, the town's librarian, had told her once that there had been a winter celebration like this since the very beginning of the town. Perhaps Captain Carter had done a service for the Snow Queen at one point. Likely Molly would never know.

One more deep breath to settle the butterflies in her stomach and she moved forward, Schrodinger pacing her as she stepped through the trees, down a cleared path to a set of double doors that only appeared on this one night every year. The doors swung open as they approached, and Molly heard Schrodinger's amazed thoughts as he saw the immense clearing for the first time.

The floor was snowy marble, not slick but terribly pale, and tall pine trees ringed the room. Although the night sky, ablaze with stars, was the only ceiling, the ambient temperature in the room was pleasant, and Molly slipped off her wrap without a thought, handing it to the one of the silent butlers that stood by the doors. The room was lit by faery lights that floated among the trees, bright enough that people were clearly visible, but not so brilliant as to dim the stars above. The air was redolent with the scents of pine and clear, crisp snow.

"Holy shit, you were right. That is definitely NOT a Molly dress."

Molly turned and grinned at the Terrible Trio, and then did a full spin. Carefully, so she didn't step on the small train. "I told you I went all out."

"You weren't kidding." Lai circled her, looking amazing herself in a little black dress that shimmered in the light. "It's strapless. And has a train. And holy shit, Molly, where did you find it?"

"You look like a faery princess," Sue told her, glowing in her own dark crimson dress. "If SA doesn't fall at your feet when he sees you, he's not worth it."

"I think all three of her admirers will be falling at her feet," Noemi said, adjusting the sleeve of her blue bolero jacket and nodding over Molly's left shoulder. "If they can move, that is."

Molly turned and saw what she was looking at. Drew, Tom, and Luke were standing by themselves in a group, staring at her with open mouths. She smiled sweetly and waved, then turned back to her friends before she started laughing. "I guess the dress worked," she said, more than a little smugly.

Are they okay? Schrodinger asked, looking back at the guys.

"They will be, as soon as the blood equalizes," Lai said, linking arms with Molly. Off they went, Schrodinger trailing behind them, still a little confused, to one of the tables scattered around the edge of the dance floor. Molly barely had time to take a sip of her champagne before Luke showed up.

"Can I have this dance?" he asked, and before she could answer, he'd spun her out onto the floor.

The night passed in a blur for Molly. She went from partner to partner, swirled in a froth of white silk and music. Drew, Luke, and Tom all paid close court, along with many others, but it wasn't until the next to last dance of the night, for which Father Christopher claimed her, that she remembered SA's note.

"I wonder who he is," she said. "I've danced with so many people tonight. I hope he got his dance."

Father Christopher smiled. "I think he might be waiting for a special song."

"Well, he doesn't have too much time left," Molly said. "The last dance is very soon." She looked over to where the Snow Queen sat on her icy throne, her pale blue eyes watching the circling dancers, a cloak of white fur clasped around her shoulders. "She'll make the call soon."

"Will you throw your shoe in?" Father Christopher asked.

"I won't have much of a choice," she said, laughing a little. "Even if I claim exhaustion, no one will let me sit out the Cinderella dance."

The final dance of the Snow Queen's Ball was always the Cinderella dance. Every woman in the room put one of her shoes in a large pile in the middle of the dance floor, and then the men in the room each chose one. Even the Snow Queen herself would put a shoe in. It was said that good luck was bestowed on the man who partnered her in the final dance. If she liked him, she would give him a shining silver star. If she really liked him, it was said, she would whisper in his ear, granting him a single favor. Molly had seen her give several men a kiss on the cheek, but never whisper to anyone, not in all the years she'd been going to the ball. She wondered who would be lucky enough to dance with the Snow Queen tonight.

When the song ended, the Snow Queen lifted her hands, and the musicians nodded. She stood up, shrugging off her fur wrap to show a shimmering white gown with silver and green accents on it that matched the delicate crown on her white hair, and everyone in the ball room turned to see what she had to say.

"My friends, thank you once again for helping me grace the Yule season with music and dance," the Snow Queen said, her sweet voice carrying throughout the room. She looked maybe seventeen, although Molly knew she was older. Perhaps immortal, even; the Snow Queen was definitely not human, although whether she truly was the Spirit of Winter, as some said, was questionable. "As is custom, the final dance will be the Cinderella dance. Ladies?"

And she stepped down from her throne, glided to the middle of the floor like a swan on a glassy lake, and lifted her pale skirts to kick one delicate shoe off. Every woman followed suit, and Molly could only wonder who would pick up her white ballet flat from the pile of shoes. She retreated back to the table where Schrodinger waited and sat down, looking out over the crowd.

And now what? Schrodinger asked.

"Now it's the guys' turn," Molly told him. "They'll choose a shoe, and find the lady who it belongs to. That's their partner for the final dance."

Oh, that's odd. The CrossCat settled back down on the cushion that one of the butlers had brought out for him, watching the men go in and take a shoe from the large pile.

For a few minutes, the ballroom buzzed with noise as they tried to find who had the mate to the shoe in their hands.

Molly watched Tom approach, but the white shoe in his hand had a kitten heel and she shook her head, watching his face fall. Luke followed him, but the delicate crystal shoe in his hands was far too small to fit on Molly's foot. She shook her head again and pointed to the throne. "I think you're a lucky man tonight, Luke."

His shoulders actually sagged for a minute. "I'd rather it be you, honestly," he said, then winked at her and turned, walking up to the throne. The Snow Queen held out her foot, and he slipped the shoe on, smiling up at her.

"Lucky bastard," Molly heard, and turned to see Drew standing beside her. He wasn't looking at Luke, though; he was looking at her, and the white ballet flat peeking out from under her skirts. He held its mate in his hands and knelt down, slipping his hand under her dress to draw out her bare foot. His fingers skimmed along her calf as he did so, and Molly caught her breath at the sensations. Then, once the shoe was on, he stood up and offered her his hand.

Tonight, he'd traded in his normal blue jeans and simple tee-shirts for a suit and jacket in dark blue. As they took their places on the floor, Drew set one hand on her waist, and took her hand with his other. She placed her hand on his shoulder. And, as always, the band started to play "The Christmas Waltz."

"I'm glad you saved me a dance," he murmured, and Molly's lips quirked in a smile.

"I saved you several," she said.

"I know, but this was the one I wanted." They danced in silence for a few more measures, her head resting on his chest, his cheek against her curls. She'd lost most of the sparkling stars the hairdresser had put in, but true to the woman's claims, the elaborate braiding hadn't moved all night.

For Molly, the rest of the dancers on the floor vanished. It was just her and Drew, moving in the ancient steps of the waltz as the musicians played their hearts out. And as they danced, she realized two things. One, how safe she felt cradled in his embrace.

Two, just how far her heart had gone. It no longer mattered who SA was. Molly had made her choice, and she surrendered utterly to it.

She didn't hear the music stop. Neither did Drew, apparently, because they continued to dance until someone tapped him on the shoulder. Then they both jumped. There before them stood the Snow Queen.

"I'm so sorry..." Drew began, but she smiled gently at him, cutting him off with a shake of her head.

"Sorry? Why? Because you have fallen under the spell of the music? Do not apologize for that. I just wish I could allow you to dance here all night, but I must return to my realm. You can continue this dance, but not here."

He looked down at Molly, who smiled. "I've got a lovely kitchen we can dance in."

"Then let's go dance."

Snoopy and the Red Baron
Sunday, December 19

Molly was singing in the kitchen. Schrodinger lay snuggled in his cat bed in the tea room next to the wood stove and listened to her. When she was happy, he was happy. And she was most definitely happy today.

This had been the first Snow Queen's Ball Schrodinger had attended, although he'd heard stories of them before. Everyone who lived or traveled the Roads near Carter's Cove had heard stories of the famous winter party, and his uncle had actually lived in the Winter Palace for a few years as a part of the Snow Queen's entourage. He thought over last night, especially how Molly had danced and danced, her face alight with enjoyment, and how beautiful the music had been. Schrodinger loved music, all types, and the Snow Queen's musicians were the best he'd ever heard, with the exception of Darian.

There had even been some other travelers there, including one of his old friends from childhood, and Schrodinger had had the chance to get some news from his home. His sister had had another litter, and he wondered if he should try and get back to the Den for a few days to visit.

Maybe after the new year, he thought, shifting a bit. *Once I'm sure*

Molly's all set.

She and Drew had stayed up late, so the fact that she was singing in the kitchen was a bit amazing to him. He'd gone to bed when they'd gotten home, but she and Drew had stayed up, dancing and drinking tea in the kitchen until the wee hours of the morning. If fact, he wasn't actually sure if she'd slept at all. She'd woken him up at 5:30 am and they'd done breakfast together, then come down to the store. Drew had already been gone.

Now Schrodinger wondered what would happen next. He liked Drew. Molly obviously liked Drew. But there was still the problem – was Drew SA? Or was SA someone else? If he was someone else, would Molly still choose Drew? Schrodinger heaved a sigh.

That's an awfully heavy sigh, another voice said, and Schrodinger looked up as a large black dog with an adorable four-year-old girl in tow came ambling over to him. He willingly moved over to let Jack flop down with him on the bed; Aunt Margie had invested in the large size, so there was plenty of room for all three of them. Lily laid down between her two friends, snuggling in.

"What's wrong, Schrodinger?" she asked, stroking his soft head. "You shouldn't look this sad. It's almost Christmas!"

Not sad, Schrodinger assured her. *Just a little worried, that's all.*

Why? Jack asked. *What is there to be worried about?*

Molly. Schrodinger told them about SA, and the cards with the Christmas carols, and the three Gate techs. And then he told them about what happened at the Ball. *So now I'm worried that she won't want to choose SA if he's not Drew, or that somehow we've messed it up,* he finished, putting his head back down on his front paws. *What if this isn't what Santa wanted to have happen? What if SA is someone else completely, and it's not someone that's good for her?*

"Then she won't choose him," Lily said, with complete confidence. "She's good like that."

Besides, do you really think Santa won't have been keeping a close eye on this? Jack added. *He's SANTA. And he rules December. You know he wouldn't let this get out of hand.*

Not really. This is my first Christmas, after all, Schrodinger reminded them. *Remember? CrossCats don't celebrate Christmas.*

"Really?" Lily blinked. "What do you celebrate then?"

Winter Solstice, he said. *We light a fire in the morning, and keep it lit all through the day and the night, so the sun will come back. There are presents given at the end of the day, but not from Santa. From family and friends, to celebrate the dawning of a new year.*

"Sounds like our home," Lily said. "Mommy and Daddy have been very busy getting the house ready. Grandma and Grandpa are coming up! Mommy's in now, getting some last minute Christmas presents." She leaned in and whispered, "I think she's getting Grandpa another book. And some tea."

Molly said she was ordering cookies too, Schrodinger said. *Special ones, but she wouldn't tell me what kind.*

Lily squealed and clapped her hands together in delight, while Jack thumped his tail. *Molly's cookies are the best!*

Schrodinger was about to respond when he saw Aunt Margie go into the kitchen. In her hands was a familiar red envelope, and he sighed again.

What? Jack said.

What if she's not happy with who SA is? Schrodinger said. *What if she feels she has to accept him, and he breaks her heart? What if…*

Jack thumped his tail again, cutting the CrossCat off. *You can play the what-if game all you want, and make yourself crazy,* the hound said. *Or you can enjoy the season and trust that Santa has everything well in hand. I suggest the second alternative.*

You are wise, Schrodinger agreed. *I think--*

A squeal of absolute joy cut through his thought, and all three of them looked to the kitchen door. Schrodinger could just see Molly, who was spinning around, clutching something in her hands. *Come on! Let's go see what it is,* he said.

They all bounded into the kitchen, arranging themselves in front of Molly. "What is it?" Lily asked eagerly. "Did you get a good present from SA?"

"I did!" Molly said, laughing at the hopeful faces in front of her. "Would you guys like a cookie, and then I'll show you?"

"Yes!" Three voices chorused, and Aunt Margie, who had moved to the side of the kitchen as they tumbled in, laughed as well. Molly turned and took three sugar cookies sparkling with icing and colored sugar from the rack behind her and gave them each one. Once they were settled with their treats, she picked up the red envelope from the island and opened it again.

"Look," she said, pulling out the most glorious snowflake Schrodinger had ever seen. It shimmered and glowed in her hand, sending off little sparks of magical light. "SA sent me one of the Snow Queen's own snowflakes for our tree! Isn't it amazing?"

It was. The Snow Queen rarely gave away her snowflakes, and those who got them rightly treasured them. It took very old magic to enlarge a single snowflake and make it last forever, Schrodinger knew. Molly had been given an amazing gift.

Jack nudged Schrodinger and said quietly, *I don't think you have anything to worry about. The Snow Queen and Santa are very close, so I've heard, and this proves that she, at least, approves of SA. She always knows who gets her snowflakes.*

True. But Schrodinger still didn't know if that soothed his mind. Luke was the one who had danced with the Snow Queen, not Drew, and no one had seen her give the snowflake out. What if Luke had sent this? Would Molly still be happy with him? Or would she go with someone else?

He shook his head, and reminded himself that he had to have faith. It would work out.

"What does the note say?" Aunt Margie prodded her, bringing Schrodinger back to the present.

"It says, 'Here's a present to remind you of last night. Thank you for saving me a dance. Now, I feel like I could fight the world. SA'" Molly looked at the snowflake, her eyes shining. "As if I could ever forget."

<><>

"Hey, you got a minute?"

Tom looked up from his plate as Drew dropped into the chair opposite him. The Gate Station had a small dining room/kitchen where the staff could theoretically cook if needed. Luckily for them, the Cove supplied the Station with plenty of ready-made meals that could be heated or eaten cold. Tom had found some cold cuts, and a plate of Molly's rolls, and made himself some sandwiches after he came off shift. Now, he shrugged. "Free country," he said, picking up a sandwich. "Frankly, I'm surprised to see you here."

"Why?" Drew asked, sipping at the mug of tea in his hand.

"Because I figured you'd still be at Molly's." Tom couldn't quite keep the bitterness out of his voice, even though he was trying, and bit at the sandwich rather than say anything else.

"Molly had to work this morning, so she kicked me out around 2," Drew said. "And nothing happened, other than talking and dancing."

An image of Molly and Drew dancing in the same kitchen he and Molly used to dance in ran through Tom's mind, and the sandwich turned to dust in his mouth. He set it back down, forcing himself to swallow the bite he'd taken. "Sounds like you had a good time," he said, after taking a drink from his cup.

"We did." Drew watched him for a long moment, and then said, "It's not over yet."

"Are you sure?" Tom got up and dumped the sandwich into the trash, and rinsed off his plate. "It looked pretty settled to me, and to everyone else."

"You knew this could happen," Drew said. "We all agreed to it. Besides, she's got to make her own decision."

"I know." Tom leaned against the sink, looking out the window at the snow falling over the Cove. "I know."

But knowing it intellectually and seeing it happen were two different things. Tom grit his teeth, trying to force the jealousy down.

"Tom--"

"Look, I'm fine," Tom interrupted, turning back around. "I'm just tired, and I don't want to talk about it right now. She'll make her decision, if she hasn't already. I know the rules. Don't worry about me."

But as he walked out of the kitchen, Tom wondered if he could let go. *I think I'll have to just go for it,* he thought, climbing the stairs to his room. *I need to talk to her. Tomorrow, I think.*

And if she tells you no? A tiny voice in the back of his head asked. *What then?*

"I'll worry about that then," Tom said out loud to his reflection in the mirror on the wall. It stared back at him, unconvinced.

It's the Most Wonderful Time of the Year
Monday, December 20

Molly looked out over the packed tea room and sighed. Not surprisingly, the bookstore had been rocking all day; it was only five days until Christmas, and no one was immune to the last minute Christmas panic. Molly herself still had a few things to buy, but she figured she'd hit the stores on Tuesday. She needed to finish filling Schrodinger's stocking, pick up his big Christmas present, and she wanted to get something special for SA. Especially since she was pretty certain she knew who he was.

And if it wasn't him, then she still needed the gift. She'd just give it to him anyway.

Behind her, the oven timer dinged. Normally, Molly didn't even bother with the timer, but her senses were a bit overwhelmed by the sheer number of people surging in and out of her domain. Now, she turned to the oven and pulled out yet another tray of gingerbread men to add to the army marching around the kitchen. One more tray was waiting to go in; she put them in the oven, reset the timer, and then went into the pantry for icing supplies.

When she came out, Tom was waiting in the kitchen for her. Molly had heard the footsteps and her heart had swelled a bit; when she saw who it was, she couldn't help but feel a little spurt of disappointment. Then she reminded herself that Drew did have to work, after all. She couldn't expect him to dance attendance on her all the time.

"Hi," she said, smiling up at Tom. "How's it going?'

"It's going." Tom looked a bit ill at ease, and tired, and Molly's smile slipped a little in concern. "Molly, can we talk?"

"We are talking," she said, putting the supplies she'd gathered on the island and moving to the sink. "What's on your mind?"

He hesitated, watching her draw a glass of water, and then said, "I want to talk to you about us."

"What about us? We're friends," Molly said, coming back over to the island with the water. She poured powdered sugar and meringue powder into the bowl, then began adding water and beating the mixture with a wooden spoon.

"I want us to be more than friends."

She sighed, not stopping her mixing. "I'm not sure that's possible any more, Tom. You're not going to change, and I can't live with your weird silences and your secrets. You lost your chance to let me in." Molly didn't look up at him. "I'm happy with being friends, and I don't want to lose that. I like you. I even love you, but I'm realizing it's like a sister loves a brother."

"And there's nothing I can do to change that?" Tom's voice was strained, a little desperate, and Molly's heart broke a little.

"No." She finally put the spoon aside and looked up at him. "You had your chance, Tom. I'm sorry. I can't go through that again." She picked up the red food coloring and dripped six drops into the frosting. "Please don't ask me to."

"You know that Drew will be gone, just like I was."

"Yes, I do." She looked back up and stared steadily at him. Not angrily, she realized; there was no anger left in her. Just sadness. "But I don't think Drew will vanish when he's not being sent out to fix a Gate or find a traveler, and think I won't figure it out."

Tom had the decency to flush at that. "It wasn't what you were thinking."

"How could I know what to think, Tom? You never told me anything. And then that girl called. And you wouldn't talk about it. What was I supposed to think?" Molly took a second bowl and began to make green icing. "But it doesn't matter now. I don't really care who she is, or what happened. I'm just not letting you back into my life that deeply again. Schrodinger and I deserve better than that."

"I don't know if I can just be friends, Molly."

"I'm sorry. I'll miss you, but that's all I can offer you." She mixed up a third bowl of icing and left it white, then she pulled out three pastry bags from the drawer in the island.

"Molly, please, give me one more chance." Tom put his hand over hers, and Molly's jaw tightened. "Please."

"No." Molly pulled her hand away. "I'm sorry, Tom. I can't. All we can be is friends."

"Everything I've done this month, everything I've helped them with, has been to show you I've changed, to win you back," he said, and she stared at him. "I was hoping for a Christmas miracle, but I won't get that, will I?"

"Everything you've done?" She had a sinking suspicion she knew what he meant, and it didn't bode well for either of them.

He shook his head and stuffed his hands into his pockets. "Never mind. It was stupid. I'm stupid. Forget I said anything." Then, before she could say anything else, Tom fled the kitchen.

Molly watched him go, her mind whirling. It wasn't too hard to guess what he'd meant by "everything he'd done," but what had he meant by everything he'd helped them with? Helped who? Was SA perhaps more than one person?

Then Molly shook her head and filled the pastry bags. It didn't matter, really. She'd know everything by Friday, and she'd already made up her mind.

Schrodinger came trotting in about thirty minutes later, carrying the familiar red envelope in his mouth. He waited until she laid down the icing bag and then put his front paws on her leg, offering the envelope to her.

"I'd wondered where that was," Molly said, slipping her finger under the flap and opening the envelope. The CD and scrap of paper came out into her hand, along with another ornament. This one was delicate brass, and it shimmered in the light.

"Oh, how pretty," Molly breathed, enchanted. The dark mood that the conversation with Tom had conjured vanished as she gazed at the gift.

What is it? Schrodinger asked, jumping up onto a stool to see better.

"It's a triskelion," Molly said, showing him. There was scrolling knotwork along each of the arms. "A symbol of eternity, since it has no beginning or end." She traced her fingertip along it, feeling the etchings.

What does the note say?

She laid the ornament back down gently and picked the note up. "Dear Molly, I'm hoping this is a symbol of what we have before us. A love that lasts forever. But even if not, this Christmas season has been a magical one. Thank you. SA"

Schrodinger looked over at her. *Tom was here.*

"Yes, he was."

He didn't look happy when he left.

Molly sighed, and slipped the CD in to the stereo. "No, he wasn't. He wanted me to give him another chance to be together. And when I told him no, he…well, he took it better than I thought he would."

Schrodinger slipped down from his stool and padded over to her, rubbing his head against her leg. *That's not all, is it?*

"No." Molly picked him up, snuggling him against her cheek. "I don't think SA is a single person, and I'm afraid that this might end badly after all."

Because if you choose one of them, the others might be hurt.

"At least one of them will be." Molly remembered the anguish in Tom's eyes with a pang. "I just hope he doesn't do anything stupid."

Schrodinger purred comfortingly in her ear. *You can't protect him from himself, Molly. It's up to Tom how he responds to your choice.*

"I know. I know." Molly cuddled the CrossCat up to her. "I know."

But knowing and accepting it were two different things.

<><>

"Hey, where's Tom?" Mal asked, sticking his head in to the TV room, where Drew and Luke had their heads bent over a book of maps. "Isn't he in here?"

Luke and Drew exchanged confused looks. "I thought he was on duty," Drew said.

Mal swore, nearly losing the cigarette in his mouth. "He's supposed to be, but there's no one at the board. I know you just came off, Luke, but I need one of you--"

"I'll do it," Drew said. "I'm due to go on in about two hours anyways."

"Thank you. We've got two different shipments that are due in any minute, and no one knows where they are." Mal stomped out, muttering under his breath.

Drew and Luke exchanged another look, and Drew got up.

"What do you think he's done?" Luke asked him, closing the book and revealing the red envelopes. "Do you think he's gone over to see her?"

"Probably." Drew shook his head, and counted the envelopes again. "Today's is missing, so I wouldn't be surprised."

"But it was supposed to be given to Father Christopher..." Luke trailed off as Drew shrugged.

"Give Father a call, but I'll bet he never got it. I just hope Tom hasn't done something really stupid." Then he hustled out the door, before Mal came back looking for him.

Luke joined him as the second caravan came rumbling through the Gate. "You were right," the other tech said quietly. "Father Christopher said Tom called him and told him he would take care of things."

Drew swore under his breath as he watched the sleek train slow to a halt and stop, blowing steam into the air. "He's a damn idiot."

"Yes," Luke agreed, as they watched several large packages come out of one of the cars. Drew glanced at the log, and began to punch in the next destination for the train. "But Aunt Margie said Molly got the envelope, and the store is still standing, so hopefully he didn't blow everything."

"We're almost done," Drew said, shaking his head. "You'd think he'd know better than to screw it up now."

Luke didn't say anything to that, and Drew looked over at him. "What?" he asked.

"Look, Drew, I've known Tom a long time," Luke said, still staring out at the train. "And I know how he looked at the ball."

"Nothing happened there, I told you both," Drew said.

Luke held up a hand. "I know. And I know that Molly's pretty much made up her mind. But Tom doesn't take defeat well." He finally looked at Drew. "Just warning you."

"Warning me?" Drew's stomach dropped a bit. "He wouldn't."

"I hope not." Luke sighed. "But he loves Molly."

Drew turned back to the board, chilled. This could get bad. Really bad. And they hadn't thought of that.

The Christmas Song
Tuesday, December 21

Molly stepped outside and breathed in deeply. The icy scent of snow, evergreens, and the sea flooded her lungs, giving her a blast of energy that she never tired of. In the Cove, the combination of Roads and the sea gave the air a fresh smell that she didn't notice in other towns. *Maybe it's the magic,* she thought once again. It was the only answer she could come up with. After all, the folks in the Cove had cars; not that many of them used them in town, true, but they were there. And there were always tourists.

Then again, most towns you don't see sleighs on a regular basis, she reminded herself, watching as Lisa and Neil Jackson glided by over the icy paving stones, pulled by two of the stags from the herd they kept on their farm. The pale white deer looked like snow ghosts as they trotted down the lane, heading into the downtown area. Waving to Lisa as the sleigh went past, Molly made a mental note to package up some more of the gingerbread men and send them off to the farm; the family would love them. And she'd include some of her special doggie cookies too, for Tigger, yet another one of Schrodinger's friends.

"I love this town," she said out loud, shifting her backpack to her left shoulder. "I don't really think I could live anywhere else."

Schrodinger was upstairs, still sleeping – she'd left without him, telling him that she couldn't very well Christmas shop for him if he was right there with her. Her plan had been to borrow Aunt Margie's car and drive into Portland, but Molly found herself loathe to leave the Cove on this perfect morning, when the sun was shining. Instead she walked by the bookstore and into the very center of town, where it looked like Christmas had exploded all over everything. She'd been so busy with the tea shop that this was her first trip this year into the center square, and she paused at the edge of it, fascinated.

Carter's Cove had a few different "town squares." The one with the Town Hall and the Courthouse was a few streets over, but the acknowledged center of town was called Captain's Square, and was where the shops held sway. In the center, there was a large statue of a centaur looking out over the buildings: a monument to Calypso, one of the first merchant sea captains after Captain Carter to sail into the Cove. She and her crew had helped explore one of the Sea Roads to the Eastern Kingdoms, bringing back tea and silk among other things. Molly's mother had a beautiful spider silk tapestry from one of Calypso's final voyages hanging in her office. Now, Calypso's statue was wreathed in greenery, with small white lights twinkling in between the leaves. At her feet were eight small trees, lit with the same lights, marking off the cardinal points of the compass. Each tree was decorated in a different way, signifying the eight holidays in the centaurs' Wheel of the Year, and were donated by Calypso's descendants, some of whom still lived in the Cove.

The stores themselves went all out in an effort to spread the Christmas cheer. Instead of decorating right after Halloween and using canned Christmas music (which Molly detested), the stores in Captain's Square didn't decorate until the weekend after Thanksgiving, and most used the music of local artists or played WCOV. Some stores even had live players come in. Molly smiled and looked around, plotting her trip.

She needed more stuff for Schrodinger, of course, and the rest of her family. And she wanted to get some special tins to fill for the

Gate techs who had made her Christmas so special already.

Thinking about that made her recall her conversation with Tom the day before, and she sighed. *I hope we can still be friends,* Molly thought, heading into the first store on her list. *But it's up to him. I won't be more.*

Home For All was the Cove's answer to the Blue Seal stores Molly had seen in other towns, but Julia Kasey, who ran the store, had refused repeated offers to franchise.

"They just don't cater to the clients I have," she'd said one time to Molly. "I mean, CrossCats are just the beginning – and they don't even need special food. Have you seen what manticores eat, for example? Or Spot?"

"Who has a pet manticore in the Cove?" Molly had asked. "I want to know, so I can avoid their place."

Julia had laughed at that. "One of the dwarven enclaves along the Stone Road have two. Apparently they're very good at sniffing out precious metals."

"Maybe, but I think I'll still pass," Molly had said.

Home For All also carried the special treats that Schrodinger adored. Molly had ordered a large package for him, along with a new winter coat for the CrossCat, since he hadn't lived through a Cove winter before. January and February were often the coldest months of the year, and she didn't want him to get sick.

"Hello!" she called out, stepping into the store. The scent of cloves and apples hit her nostrils: Julia had set up a crockpot of mulled cider on a small table near the door, with paper cups and a sign inviting folks to help themselves. Molly did, then went into the back of the store, where she found Julia packing up something that looked like chicken feed.

"It is," she said, when Molly asked her. "I do sell the stuff for Earth animals as well as the exotics, after all." She stood up, dusted her hands off, and added, "In for your order, I assume?"

"Yes," Molly said, and followed her back out to the counter, where Julia pulled out a large parcel. Molly opened it eagerly and then sighed. "Oh Julia, it's perfect."

Julia grinned. "Awesome." The super-soft material, like flannel but waterproof, was hand-woven in one of the smaller villages off the main Sea Road. This one was varied shades of blue and green, which would look stunning against Schrodinger's mackerel-grey stripes. Molly folded it back up and put it in her backpack along with the treats, then headed out again after a few more minutes of chatting.

Her next stop was the Tin Shop, a lovely little store that specialized in boxes, tins, and all sorts of containers for all sorts of things. She picked out some specialty tins for cookies and then made her way up to the counter.

"Hi Molly!" Catherine Taylor greeted her, smiling. "Find everything you needed today?"

Molly nodded. "Just these for right now, but I need to talk to you about a mass order of tins for Valentine's Day. I have a feeling that I'm going to get a run of orders for chocolate raspberry truffles and chocolate strawberries again this year, and I want to be prepared. But I don't want heart-shaped. Something different."

"Oooh, put me down for a tin of each now!" Catherine said, laughing and pulling out a catalog. "What did you have in mind?"

They firmed up the order (gift boxes in gold and silver, with tiny cats holding red and pink hearts on the ribbons), and then Molly went to pay for the current crop of tins she'd picked out. She held out her debit card, but Catherine shook her head.

"You're all set," the redhead said, grinning.

"Excuse me?" Molly said, confused, and tried to hand her the debit card again.

"You're all set," Catherine repeated, refusing the card and bagging up the tins. And then she handed Molly a small red envelope with a package attached to it. "Apparently someone anticipated your need."

Molly raised an eyebrow but opened the envelope. "Dear Molly, I know you'll need some more tins, so these are on me. You always do this time of year. And a special treat for you to introduce Schrodinger to later. SA"

She then looked closely at the package, and laughed. "Chestnuts.

Of course."

After stowing the chestnuts and card in her backpack, she bade Catherine a farewell and headed back out. The sun was starting to hide behind the clouds, and Molly could smell snow again. And something else that made her stomach rumble: chocolate.

"I deserve a treat," she said to herself, heading in the direction of Katarina and Mick's coffee shop, called the Vienna Lady's Cafe. Luckily for her, they served delicious hot chocolate as well as coffee, made with Katarina's well-guarded recipe from her homeland in Vienna. As Molly stepped into the shop, she inhaled deeply.

"Molly! Come in and try this new treat!" Mick's Scottish accent tickled her ears. "It's a secret family recipe that I finally convinced me mam to give up."

"How can I refuse that?" Molly said, grinning. "As long as it doesn't involve coffee."

"Nope. Although there is a wee bit of Scottish whiskey in the crust." Mick winked at her.

Molly's eyebrows rose. "Do tell."

She took a seat at one of the little tables, near the Christmas tree that was decorated with tartan bows and little electric candles. Mick came out from around the glass case that took up the back wall of the cafe, carrying a tray with several dishes on it. The amazing smell of chocolate wafted from the pot and Molly groaned.

"I really need to get this recipe from her," she said, pouring herself a cup of the hot chocolate. Then she looked at one of the other dishes. "Is that trifle?"

"No," Mick said, sitting down opposite from her and grinning. "It's cranachan."

Molly looked closely at it, inspecting the crystal glass. It certainly looked like trifle, with layers of cream and jewel-toned raspberries. Mick handed her a spoon, and she dipped it in.

The sharp taste of whiskey, mellowed by the sweet raspberries and rich cream, exploded in her mouth. Molly's eyes widened.

"Good, eh?" Mick chuckled as she dipped the spoon back in.

"We should do this, yes?"

"Oh yes," Molly agreed. "But it tastes like the alcohol isn't cooked off."

"No," he said. "This is an adults-only dessert. You soak the oats in good whiskey overnight before you assemble everything." Mick got up, carefully adjusting his kilt. "I'll leave you to enjoy."

Molly did just that, watching the people go by as she sipped the chocolate and finished off the cranachan. She didn't often get time to just sit by herself. *I should make time for this more often,* she thought. Her gaze strayed to the backpack on the floor, and the chestnuts inside. *Such a thoughtful gift. I really do need to thank all of them.*

That thought triggered another one. *I'm really lucky. I have three of the best guys in the world willing to make my Christmas a memorable one. How did I get that lucky?*

Unfortunately, she didn't have an answer to that.

The Twelve Days of Christmas
Wednesday, December 22

"Schrodinger, hurry up! We want to start!" Sarah called from the tea room, and Molly laughed.

"Go!" she said, shooing the CrossCat off his stool. "I'll finish these. It's sounds like they're waiting for you. And you've been waiting for this."

Schrodinger didn't need much encouragement. He hopped down and shot out of the room like he'd been stung by something. Molly laughed again, turning her attention back to the tea cakes cooling on the rack on the sideboard. She and Schrodinger had been trying to decide how to decorate them, and she still wasn't sure.

She'd adapted her gingerbread recipe, making it into fluffy cupcake-sized tea cakes, a little spicier and less sweet than normal cupcakes. Now she chewed on her lower lip as she pondered options. Frost them with a cream cheese frosting? Dust with powdered or cinnamon sugar? Stud with candied orange and lemon and cherries? A combination of the three? Decisions, decisions…

"Are you expecting them to do something?" Drew asked from behind her. "Like talk, or do tricks? Because if that's the case, I'm not sure I want to eat them, and they look really tasty."

"I hope not," Molly said, turning around and grinning at him. "Because then I think I'd be violating a bunch of international and inter-Realm laws. I'm pretty sure that would be illegal to sell sentient cupcakes."

"You've made sentient cupcakes?" he asked, coming around the island and pulling her into his arms. "I've fallen in love with a goddess!"

"Hardly. Just a kitchen witch." His words made her glow.

"You are not 'just' anything," Drew said, dropping a light kiss on her upturned lips. "So why were you staring at cupcakes?"

"I'm trying to decide how to finish them," she said. "They're gingerbread, and I'm torn between them with cinnamon sugar, candied fruit, or cream cheese frosting."

He frowned at the cupcakes as she reluctantly extricated herself from his arms. "I dunno, the cream cheese sounds good, but a bit heavy."

"That's what I was thinking." Molly sighed. "But they need something."

"What about the glazed icing you did on the gingerbread men?" Drew suggested. "With maybe some candied fruit on top?"

Molly blinked. "I hadn't even considered that," she admitted, tilting her head to one side as she thought. "That could work."

Moving almost on auto-pilot as her brain worked through the idea, she went into the pantry. "Would you like some tea?" she called out, almost as an afterthought. "The kettle's hot."

"When isn't it?" Drew teased, and then added, "Unfortunately, I don't have a lot of time today." Molly stuck her head out of the pantry, raising an eyebrow at him, and he explained, "I'm heading out for a few days. Gotta go fix a Gate near Caledon. The order just came in, and it's my turn."

"But Friday's Christmas Eve!" she said. "I was hoping..." and then she bit her lip and stopped.

"Hey, hey, hey, don't look like that." Drew came into the pantry and slipped his arms around her. "You spend Christmas with your family, right? Do you think they'd mind me crashing there, if I came in late Christmas Eve?"

Since she'd already checked with her mother, Molly could shake her head. "Of course not. They would love to have you. And Schrodinger will be ecstatic."

"Good." He kissed the top of her head. "Then I'll head out now, and I'll see you Christmas Eve."

Molly gave him a sideways look from under her eyelashes. "Having left tomorrow's SA gift with one of your co-conspirators?"

"I don't know what you're talking about," Drew said innocently, but there was a mischievous sparkle in his green eyes.

"Sure you don't," Molly said, her lips twitching into a smile. Then she sighed. "Be careful?"

"I will. It should be a fast fix. Some idiot got the Gate stuck in the open position, and they've been having issues with one of the other Realms nearby, the Midden, so it needs to be closed asap." He kissed her gently again. "I promise, we'll be in and out."

"You'd better be." Molly gave in and hugged him fiercely. "We'll both be looking for you Christmas Eve."

"Maybe I'll find something for your Christmas present there," he said.

"You're the only Christmas present I want," Molly admitted, and he responded the way she hoped he would: drawing her even closer for a long, deep kiss.

Then he was gone. Molly stood in the pantry and watched him go out the front door, then noticed the package on the island. On top of it was a familiar red envelope.

"This is my favorite Christmas movie ever, Molly. I hope you and Schrodinger enjoy it. SA"

She opened the package to find a copy of *White Christmas* on DVD. "This has to be Drew," she said out loud. "Because I can't see either Luke or Tom watching this." In fact, Tom pretty much hated most movies, since he didn't like to sit still for long periods of time.

Watching what? Schrodinger asked, coming back into the kitchen, his eyes bright. There were bits of paper stuck to his fur, and he looked like he'd rolled in a pile of scraps.

"The movie SA left for us," Molly said, covering her mouth with a hand to hide her smile. "Is Sarah's paper chain done?"

Not yet, but I had an idea for the cupcakes, and wanted to tell you, Schrodinger said. Then he sniffed. *I smell Drew!*

"He was here briefly."

And then he left? Without saying hi? Schrodinger's tail and ears drooped. *Doesn't he like me anymore?*

"Of course he does!" Molly knelt down next to him, careful not to touch the sticky pieces of paper. "But he didn't have a lot of time. Mal sent him to repair a Gate. Then he's going to join us for Christmas!"

He is? Schrodinger perked up immediately. *At the house?*

"Yep." Molly nodded. "So tell me, what did you think of for the cupcakes?"

An orange icing, the CrossCat said. *Not too sweet, but it echoes the flavors of the cake.*

"Ooh, that does sound good. Drew suggested the icing, but I like the orange idea. Not juice, though." Molly stood up, put the movie and the card into the basket out of the way, and then went and grabbed an orange from the pantry. "Orange zest?"

Perfect. Now, I'm off again to help Sarah. With that, Schrodinger went back out, leaving Molly to finish her cupcakes.

The Little Drummer Boy/Peace on Earth
Thursday, December 23

*M*olly? *Why are you still up?*

Schrodinger came padding out in to the living room. Molly was curled up on the sofa under a throw her aunt had crocheted for her years ago, looking out at the snow falling softly outside. The only light came from the Christmas tree glowing in the corner.

She didn't answer him, and he came further into the room, not sure she was even awake. *Molly?*

"Have you ever been to Caledon?" The question was so quiet that he almost missed it.

No. He jumped up onto the couch and curled up in her lap. *I haven't, actually, but my sire went once. Why?*

"That's where they sent Drew," she said, stroking him almost absently. "I've never been there. Did your sire tell you anything about it?"

It was warm when he went, Schrodinger said, after thinking for a few moments. *Very green. He said it smelled alive there.*

"Drew said they were having issues with the Midden folk, so that's why the Gate had to be fixed right away." Molly looked out at the snow again. "I've never been to the Midden either, but I've met some Midden folk. They come into the tea shop once in a while, and I've bought some lovely tea from them. I can't imagine them being trouble to anyone. They seem so gentle."

Schrodinger snuggled up against her. *It's never a whole people that makes trouble; just certain parts of the population.* He paused, and then added, *I'm sure Drew's fine.*

"I hope so."

They sat and watched the snow fall for a while. Schrodinger knew she'd received an envelope from SA earlier in the day, but he hadn't seen her open it. For all he knew, it still sat on the table in the dining room.

"No," she said, when he asked her. "I opened it. The CD is already in the player. There was nothing else with it today, not even a note."

What carol did he send you?

In response, she lifted the remote to the CD player from beside her and pressed a button. As the song "The Little Drummer Boy/ Peace on Earth" filled the room, Schrodinger listened to the words and wondered again at how prescient SA had been. Then again, if Molly was right and it was Drew, of course he'd know.

He'll be back, Schrodinger said when the song ended. *Just like he promised. And he'll be fine. No one will hurt a Gate tech. They're too well-respected.*

"I hope so," Molly said, and went back to watching the falling snow.

Schrodinger snuggled down next to her, hoping he was right as well.

<><>

"Good lord, what a mess," Drew said, looking up and down at the remains of the Gate terminal. Caledon's Gate station was a large open field with several small round open-sided huts, indicative of the mild weather the Realm enjoyed year-round. Unfortunately, open-sided huts were not particularly effective at protecting equipment from being clubbed apart.

"We found it like this yesterday," the young man who had come to the Cove to report the damage said. "Luckily, we have another terminal in the town to the west, but it is not convenient for everyone."

"Never mind the fact that the Gate is open directly to the Midden, and cannot be shut," the other man, the one that had met them there that morning, said. He was older, with a weathered face and worried eyes. "Who knows what they might do?"

"I'm less worried about that, to be honest, uncle," the young man said. "The lost revenue from the traders coming through will kill us faster than the Midden."

Drew tuned out their words as they continued to argue, reaching out with his magic to feel the breaks in the spells that were wrapped around the remains of the Gate controls. Once again, the intricacies of the Gates pulled him in, erasing the outer world as he traced the spell threads, seeing where he would need to weave them back together. He had a new control panel in the trunk he'd brought with him, but first, he'd have to gather all the spell bits, and fix them.

A hand on his shoulder interrupted him. "Your pardon, technician," the young man said. Drew looked up to see they were the only two there. "I have been called away to help another elder. I should only be gone for about 30 minutes. Will you be okay here?"

"Yes, of course," Drew said, blinking up at him. "There's nothing really here for you to do anyways."

"I meant, can you protect yourself?"

Drew noticed again the blades strapped to the young man's belt, and the heavy staff he held in his hand. "I'll be fine," he assured him. "No one will attack a Gate technician."

The young Caledonian gave him a dubious look, but then shrugged. "If you are comfortable, then I will go. I will be back as soon as I can." He re-adjusted the pack on his back and trotted off in the direction of the small town that they had come through.

A small shiver ran down Drew's spine as the man disappeared into the distance. He took a moment to look around him – he was truly alone; there were not even animals grazing in the fields nearby.

Just a few of the open-sided huts, and grass. Lots of grass.

He shook his head and turned back to the console, sinking back down into a light trance as he began to trace the spell lines again. There was something odd about how they'd broken, and it was going to take him some time to figure it out.

The outside world fell away again. Drew became the Gate, seeking out ending that shouldn't be there, and reclaiming parts of the magic that had floated away. It wasn't particularly hard, normally, but something wasn't right.

Pulling out of his diagnostic trance, he frowned, first at the remains of the terminal, and then at the pulsing Gate itself. Drew got up, stretching out his legs and getting his blood moving again. Then he went over to the Gate.

Up close, he could feel the pull of the magics, and the thrumming of the Road that ran under his feet. The Road itself was a stable one, befitting a path that had connected the Midden and Caledonia for hundreds of years. He'd taken a look at the maps before he'd come out, and this was one of the older Gates they serviced.

Now, he reached out a hand. The stones of the Gate arch trembled under his touch, and he could feel more of the ends of the spell threads reach for him. Not just from this side of the Gate, though, and Drew blinked. There were broken threads on the other side as well.

That complicates things, he thought, breaking contact with the Gate and staring at it. *If both terminals are broken, that would explain the oddities I'm finding. But if it IS broken, why didn't the Midden Station report it?*

He pulled out his cell phone and called Mal. When the Station Manager answered, Drew said, "Hey, Mal, is Caledon the only terminal reporting issues?"

Keys tapped in the background. "Yep," Mal said, after a moment. "Why?"

"Because I think the Midden one might be broken too." Drew's forehead wrinkled as he continued to stare at the Gate. "Something's weird here."

"Hang on." The background noises changed as Mal went out to

the Gate Room, and Drew heard Tom's voice. "Hey, Tom, run me a diagnostic on the – which terminal in the Midden, Drew?"

Drew reached out and touched the Gate again, looking for the end of the Road. "Terminal 16," he said, after a minute. "Midden 16."

"Midden 16," Mal relayed. "That's the northern one. Might be why it hasn't been reported – it's a way station, nothing more. No real people living there." He paused, and then said, "You were right. Tom says it's offline."

"Lovely. I'm going through to see what I can find. Send a second terminal to me, just in case."

"Be careful," Mal said.

"Always." Drew shut off the phone, tucked it into his pocket, and looked for his contact. The man hadn't come back. He left a note pinned to the remains of the control panel, grabbed a few tools and then, with a deep breath, plunged into the Gate.

On Christmas Day
Friday, December 24

*D*on't worry, Molly, he'll be here.

Molly smiled down at Schrodinger, who was standing next to her as she looked out the window. He had one paw on her leg, and his whole body radiated concern. "I know," she said, letting the curtain drop. "I was actually looking out for Zette. I wanted to make sure I caught her when she delivers the mail, so I can give her the cookies we baked for her."

Oh, good! I didn't want you to worry about Drew. Schrodinger dropped back down onto his haunches and began to wash his paw.

"I'm not." And she almost believed it. There was a little knot of concern in the center of her stomach, but she was determined to ignore it. The farmhouse her parents owned on the outskirts of Carter's Cove was bright and welcoming, warm with the scents of vanilla, cinnamon, and pine, all mixed together with the smoke from the fire in the living room fireplace. There would be a buffet spread later, full of all sorts of goodies she and her sister-in-law and mother had made over the last 24 hours, and bottles of her brother's crisp hard cider. Lily and Jack and Schrodinger were already planning how early they were going to get up the next morning, and Molly looked forward to hearing her father say, as he'd said to her and Nathan every year when they were younger, "Go back to bed, it's not 6 am yet!"

She looked outside again as she heard something scrape, and this time, she saw the mail carrier heading up the front walk. Molly took the brightly-wrapped package from the table next to her, shrugged into her coat, and opened the front door. Schrodinger started to follow her out, but then Lily called his name, and he took off up the stairs to her bedroom.

"Merry Christmas, Zette!" she said, when the mail carrier mounted the front steps. Her parents' house had a huge wraparound porch and this year, it was decorated with a snowman and Christmas greenery.

"Merry Christmas, Molly!" Zette said, smiling up at her. "Have the kids driven you guys nuts yet?"

"They're working on it," Molly admitted, offering the package to her. "I don't think we've put Lily, Jack, and Schrodinger in this many time outs in a long time."

Zette's smile broadened into a grin as she accepted the package. "I think I know what Santa's helpers get in our house tonight, and thank you! Here's the mail for you guys."

"Did the letter come?" Molly asked, flipping through the envelopes eagerly.

"Of course," Zette said. "Did you think he would forget?"

Molly squealed as she found the envelope she was looking for. "Thanks, Zette! You're the best! Have a good Christmas!" She gave the mail carrier a quick hug and then ran inside. "Lily! Jack! Schrodinger! You have mail!"

The three of them came tumbling down the stairs, all ribbons and ponytails and velvet. "What? Who sent us something?" Lily demanded.

"I don't know! But it has your names on it!" Molly shed her coat. "Come on in to the living room and we'll read it!"

They ended up snuggled together on the sectional, Lily in her lap and Jack and Schrodinger on either side of her. The large living room was dominated on one side by the large fieldstone fireplace, hung with stockings, flanked by built-in bookcases. The other end held the large Christmas tree, surrounded by a literal wall of presents. The sectional hugged one edge of the wall and then curved around towards the fireplace. The tree, decorated with the ornaments Molly's parents had collected over the years, glowed with multicolored lights. The angel that smiled down from the top of the tree had been made by Molly's mother when Molly was only Lily's age.

"Who sent us mail, Molly?" Lily asked, looking at the envelope in her hand.

"Open it and find out," Molly said. Lily opened the envelope carefully, the tip of her tongue peeking out of the corner of her mouth. She pulled the letter out and handed it to Molly.

"Dear Lily, Jack, and Schrodinger," Molly read. "Thank you so much for your letters! Mrs. Claus and I read them very carefully, and then we looked to see how good you've been. You've been doing very well, but don't forget to be good tonight too! I have to finish packing my sleigh soon, but I wanted to make sure that I wrote back to you. Don't forget to leave me some of your Aunt Molly's cookies – I love them! Oh, Rudolph asks that you leave him and the other reindeer some carrots, too. Can you do that? Thank you and Merry Christmas! Love, Santa."

Lily laughed and clapped her hands in delight. "Santa did get our letters! He wrote us back! That's so cool!" She hopped off Molly's lap. "Come on, guys, we have to go find carrots!"

All three of them tore off towards the kitchen while Molly laughed. They nearly ran over Nathan as he was coming into the room; he had to twist out of the way to avoid a collision. "I take it the letter came?" he said, handing her a glass.

"Of course it did," Molly said, taking a sip. Cider bubbled on her tongue. "Oh, this is lovely, Nathan."

He was about to answer when they both heard boots, heavy boots, on the porch. Molly's heart leapt. Was it him? She held her breath as her brother went to answer the door, and when she heard Luke's voice, she couldn't help the brief spurt of disappointment that rushed through her. Not Drew.

"Come on in and have a drink," Nathan was saying, and Molly got up to greet her friend. "I've got a fresh batch of cider we just opened."

"I can't refuse that," Luke said, giving her his shy smile. "Hi, Molly."

"Hi, Luke," she said, and then couldn't help herself. "Drew back yet?"

"Not yet," he said, smiling at her. "We're not expecting him until later today. It turned out to be a bigger repair than we knew – two Gates were actually down. And the Roads are busy today anyway."

"Oh, that's true," Molly agreed, kicking herself mentally. Of course the Roads were busy today. It was Christmas Eve, after all.

Luke handed her a red envelope. "I was asked to bring this to you, and since it meant I got to see you, well, it wasn't a hard request."

"Asked, huh?" Molly arched an eyebrow as she accepted the envelope. "By Drew?"

"No, actually," Luke said. "Tom was supposed to bring this one, but he asked me to do it instead."

Molly's other eyebrow rose. "Why? Afraid I might say something to him?"

"No, I think he's just not ready to admit that he's lost yet." Luke touched her cheek gently. "I can't blame him. I'm just a better loser than he is."

And then he and Nathan went out to the kitchen, leaving her standing there holding her envelope and staring after them, her eyes wide.

Molly? What did you get?

It was Schrodinger's voice that brought her back. She blinked down at him. "What?"

What did SA give you?

Molly opened the envelope. It was just the CD and the note, which said, "I'll be back for you, Molly, on Christmas Day. I promise. SA"

We Wish You a Merry Christmas
Saturday, December 25

*"**M**erry Christmas!"*

The words echoed through the house, pulling Molly from a dream in which she, Schrodinger, and Drew were walking down a Road that snaked between brightly lit Christmas trees and mounds of snow. The dream was shattered when nearly 250 pounds of cat, dog, and niece landed on her and the bed.

"Molly, he came, he came!" Lily squealed, and Molly woke up fast. "He did?"

Yes, Santa came! Schrodinger chimed in, and Jack barked eagerly. Molly's heart sank, but she grinned nonetheless at the eager faces looking up at her.

"He did, huh? Shall we go see what he left?" She let them pull her from the bed, down the stairs and into the living room, where her parents, Nathan and Corrine, her sister-in-law, were already waiting. Aunt Margie and Uncle Art would be over later, as would her cousins, to share in the massive Christmas dinner Mrs. Barrett had been planning for the last two weeks. Nathan handed her a cup of tea as she came into the room and when she raised an eyebrow at him, shook his head slightly. No Drew. Molly sighed.

"He'll be here," Nathan murmured to her. "It's only 6 am, after all."

"I know," she said, and then settled on the sectional to watch Lily and her comrades start to demolish the wall of presents. For the next hour, the air was filled with shreds of paper, ribbons, and the squeals of delight as presents were opened and toys were played with. Molly got some lovely gifts of her own, but she couldn't help drifting over to the window every so often and looking out at the falling snow. It was a picture-perfect Christmas Day, except for one thing.

"He'll be here," her mother said at one point, and Molly nodded.

"I know. I'm just a little worried."

Mrs. Barrett refilled Molly's tea cup and smiled at her. "Of course you are. But don't worry too much, Molly. Drew is a man of his word. He'll be here."

"That he is," Molly agreed, and turned resolutely from the window.

But the day wore on with no sign of Drew. Aunt Margie and Uncle Art showed up with more bags of presents. Her cousins Debbie and Alicia arrived soon after, bearing not only gifts but more food. And it continued to snow.

The Christmas feast was a miracle of goose, stuffing, mashed potatoes, and broccoli. The sideboard groaned under the weight of cakes and cookies, pies and puddings. Molly wondered, as she did every year, whether or not they were feeding an army or just the family.

After dinner, she took a cup of tea, slipped on her coat, and went to sit on the porch to watch the snow fall. Schrodinger joined her, resplendent in his new coat, and together they sat in silence.

You don't think he forgot, do you? Schrodinger asked softly.

"No, I don't think so," Molly said, stroking his head. "I think something happened to delay him. That happens sometimes, and Luke said it was more complicated than they'd realized. Maybe he'll be back tomorrow."

Maybe.

And then she heard it, very softly, through the falling snow. Her parents' road was nearly deserted, and she frowned. "Do you hear that?"

Bells, Schrodinger said, after a minute, raising his head. *I hear bells.*

Bells they were, and they both watched as a glow appeared down the end of the lane, cutting through the twilight snowfall. What was coming? A sleigh, Molly realized. And then her brain finally registered what her eyes were insisting she was seeing.

Not horses. Not even Lisa and Neil's stags. No, the animals pulling the sleigh coming through the snow...

Were reindeer.

"Lily! Jack! Come quick!" she shouted, jumping to her feet. "Come and see! Santa is coming!"

Because that's exactly who it was. And if he wasn't the real Santa, well, it didn't matter. He was, as the poem said, "chubby and plump, a right jolly old elf," and Molly, her tea forgotten, tore down the steps and into the lane. Sitting beside Santa was the one Christmas present she'd hoped for.

Drew leaped out of the sleigh before Santa could pull it to a halt and gathered her up in his arms. "I told you I'd be here," he said between kisses. "It just took a bit longer than I thought it would."

Schrodinger jumped up into the sleigh and looked at the jolly man in red sitting on the seat. *Thank you, Santa! It's just what I wanted!*

Santa smiled at him. "You've been a very good boy, Schrodinger," he said. "This was one delivery that I had to be there to see."

Molly, meanwhile, looked up at Drew. "Do you have an envelope for me today?" she said slyly, and he laughed.

"Of course I do! We promised you an advent calendar, didn't we? Can't forget the last day." He handed her the envelope and she pulled the flap open eagerly. The CD went into her pocket; she unrolled the parchment and read aloud the words.

"Dear Molly, we hope you enjoyed this as much as we did. Love, SA (aka Drew, Luke, and Tom)."

She kissed him again. "This has been the best Christmas ever." Then she grinned. "So, how are you going to top it next year?"

About the Author

Val Griswold-Ford is the author of the Dark Horseman novels *Not Your Father's Horseman*, *Dark Moon Seasons* and *Last Rites*, all from Dragon Moon Press. She is the co-editor (with Tee Morris) of the memorial anthology *Tales of the Tesla Ranger*. She is also the co-editor of *The Complete Guide to Writing Fantasy: the Opus Magnus* (with Tee Morris) and *The Complete Guide to Writing Fantasy: The Author's Grimoire* (with Lai Zhao), also from Dragon Moon Press, and has self-published the short e-novella *Snow* and, most recently, the short story *Convoy*. She has published several short stories in various anthologies online and in print, and is owned by three cats. She and her husband live in New Hampshire with said cats.

You can find her at www.vg-ford.com or on Twitter as @vg_ford. Her Patreon website is https://www.patreon.com/vgford, where she is releasing new fiction on a regular basis.

www.ingramcontent.com/pod-product-compliance
Lightning Source LLC
Chambersburg PA
CBHW051242170626
46809CB00004B/1446